"Slow Burn"

A Lesbian Romance

Christine L'Amour

This book is intended for Adults (ages 18+) only. The contents may be offensive to some readers. It may contain graphic language, explicit sexual content, and adult situations. May contain scenes of unprotected sex. Please do not read this book if you are offended by content as mentioned above or if you are under the age of 18. Please educate yourself on safe sex practices before making potentially life-changing decisions about sex in real life.

This story is a work of fiction. Names, characters, businesses, places, events and incidents are the products of the author's imagination or used in a fictitious manner & are not to be construed as real. Any resemblance to actual persons, living or dead, or actual events is purely coincidental. Products or brand names mentioned are trademarks of their respective holders or companies. The cover uses licensed images & are shown for illustrative purposes only. Any person(s) that may be depicted on the cover are simply models.

Edition v1.00 (2020.04.13)
www.christinelamourauthor.com

Special thanks to the following volunteer readers who helped with proofreading: Jenny, Naomi W. RB and those who assisted but wished to be anonymous. Thank you so much for your support.

Chapter One

Joanne set foot inside her new place and immediately set out again.

It wasn't that she didn't want to be there—she loved it, it was her new home—but now that she was finally here, out here, away from everything and everyone she had ever known, a stranger in this big city in the middle of the West Cost, the last thing she wanted to do was sit down and do something as ungodly as unpacking. She wanted to head out, to meet people, meet the town. And so, she did because there wasn't anyone there to tell her it was irresponsible, that it was foolish, that it was too late and she should stay in.

She stepped out onto the street and grinned up at the darkening sky. It was summer and it felt like it; not even the city could stand to be in a bad mood for long when the days lasted forever and every kid was out there screaming in delight. She picked a direction and just walked, because in a city this big she was bound to find something fast. She hadn't come from a small town, but she hadn't come from much either. This was exciting.

She had no real idea what she was doing here, 25 and having thrown her life away to be here, but that was fine. She was aggressively cheerful about the future and what it held for her. She was here; she would make it work.

It took two blocks of walking for the lights to start speckling her vision, and another few steps for it to coalesce into a fair. Joanne stared, delighted. There were stalls filled with knickknacks, handmade wooden toys and rings and necklaces, as well as some food. She had never seen a fair at night, though it made sense; most people didn't have a lot of time during the day.

She peered at stalls, focused mostly on those offering snacks. She hastily put her messy brown curls up in a ponytail so she could peer down at whatever people were cooking, without fear of it falling all over everything.

"I recommend the yakisoba two stalls to the right," came an amused voice.

Joanne blinked and straightened up, just to check if the owner of the voice was speaking to her. Apparently, yes: there was a woman standing not far away, blonde and grinning with a hand on her hip.

"Hi," Joanne said, grinning back. "I'm going to be honest; I've never had yakisoba before."

"Christ, girl, where have you been living?" the woman replied, mocking startlement. "I'm heading there right now and I guarantee it's good."

"I just moved here!" Joanne told her, excited. "I started walking and saw this little fair—I had never seen a fair at night before."

"Oh, new blood," the woman said, raising her eyebrows. "It's not such an uncommon thing. And hey, I have a tip for you if you want," she said, coming closer to whisper almost conspiratorially. "There's an awesome bar two blocks away called Jack's Spot and there's an even more awesome band playing there this Friday. You should totally go."

"Is the band yours?" Joanne asked with a laugh.

"Yeah!"

"Awesome!"

"I like you," the woman declared, then started to herd her toward the yakisoba stall. "What's your name and what are you in this humble city for? I'm Carla."

"I'm Jo, Joanne," she answered, happy. A few minutes in town and she had already made a friend; she knew moving here had been the best decision she had ever made. "I just needed some new air, I think. I'll totally come see you play; I don't have any other plans. And if you have other tips, I'm all ears—I really want to get out of the house more. Learn how to dance, go to some writing classes, watch movies, do something!"

"Dance, huh," Carla said, stroking her chin like a wise old man. "I have a friend who swears by the place where she learned salsa a few years ago. She keeps swearing she'll go back sometime soon—I could get you the info if you want."

"Carla, you're literally saving my life," Joanne said with a smile.

"Dude, we are gonna be friends!" Carla declared. "Come on, my boyfriend and some friends are sitting a little way away, let me introduce you."

"Hell yeah," Joanne said, steps light, happier than she had been in years.

***

Joanne didn't unpack. What she did was go to a store, get as many packs of instant noodles as she could so she wouldn't have to worry about food for a while, then she sat down in front of her laptop to search for those salsa lessons. She had savings to burn through and wasn't worried about cost, about rent, about getting a job—living with your parents until you were 25 padded your savings account way more than people your age were used to. So, she searched for them, and when she found them, she unrepentantly signed up for them.

And since she was still in the first excited stages of having moved out, before her spirit could be broken by a job or the sort of day-to-day worry that builds up after a while, she actually went.

***

The place was fancy without being intimidating; the lessons were given on the second floor of a building apparently dedicated to many types of dance classes. Joanne walked up the narrow flight of stairs and valiantly didn't feel insecure or, god forbid, shy. She was going to do the same thing she did at the fair: she was going to be extroverted and she was going to meet new people and perhaps even make some friends.

She arrived early. Class hadn't started yet, so she made her way to the front of the big, bare room where a man and a women were standing and chatting quietly and made to introduce herself.

"Hello," she said when she was close enough. "I'm Joanne Parker, I'm a new student. Are you two the teachers?"

"Yes, I remember getting an email from you," the woman said with a bland but polite smile. "The class will start soon, don't worry, it's early enough that you won't have missed much. I'm sure you'll catch up very soon."

"All right," Joanne said, feeling a bit awkward. The woman quickly looked away and went back to talking to the man. Joanne contained a sigh—not everyone was going to be as outgoing and nice as

Carla. She should just wait until some other students arrived.

"Hello, Vivian," came a smooth, polite voice from right behind her. "I brought the money, like I said I would. Again, apologies for not paying you sooner."

Joanne turned around.

Oh, but the woman was gorgeous. She was significantly taller than Joanne with black hair cropped short to her head; stylishly short. Her eyes were very, very dark. She looked calm and almost bored, the way terrifyingly competent people tended to look in places where they didn't need to work as hard as they were used to, and that coupled with her simple but light and smart style of clothing made Joanne immediately think: lawyer, or maybe doctor.

The woman turned and glanced at her; for some reason, Joanne felt her face flush and her mouth dry up.

"Hello," the woman said. "I haven't seen you before."

"I'm—I'm new," Joanne said, startled that the woman had spoken to her and trying not to show it. "I'm Joanne. Jo is fine. Jo Parker." She bit her lips before she could continue making a fool of herself.

"Nice to meet you," the woman said, prim and proper like a child who had just been told that is what is done when one meets someone new; like she wasn't used to saying it. "I'm Beatriz Harrington."

"Nice to see you making friends, Bea," the teacher said—the guy, not the woman—with an amused smile on his face. He didn't look mocking, per se, but close enough to it, a condescending tilt to his

8

smile. Beatriz, or Bea apparently, shrugged at him and moved back to the back of the classroom.

"So, the way we work—couples that come together stay together," he said, turning to Joanne, perhaps having realized she was indeed new and had no idea what she was supposed to do. "People who come alone—men and women—dance together but switch partners when the songs end. Since, yes, there are a few more women than men, you won't be able to dance sometimes."

Joanne raised one eyebrow. "Can't some women dance together then?"

"The lady and the gentlemen's steps are different, and what are you going to do, learn both at once?" he said, shaking his head and giving her a funny look. "The class is about to start."

Joanne accepted the cue and moved to the back of the class. Beatriz was more or less beside her, she saw. Bea was standing at the back, closer to the door, like she was already half a step out of it, wanting to not be here.

Joanne had never had so much fun in her life, which was why it was so jarring to see Beatriz so quiet, stoic-faced, and rigid; she subtly leaned away from every single man who danced with her, awkward and cold.

***

Joanne went up the stairs to her new place at a run, not caring that it was a bit late and some neighbors might complain. She had been out all day today, combing the neighborhood for a library, and needed to hurry if she was going to be on time for Carla's show at that bar nearby; she checked her phone for the time. It was five in the afternoon. She had enough time to eat something, take a shower and decide what to wear.

She had two books under her arm and she dropped them somewhat carefully on top of her minuscule coffee table when she arrived home. They were books she had never seen before; by the covers, one was some type of sci-fi clearly full of itself and the other a murder mystery, and Joanne was really looking forward to reading both. Maybe she should make a blog to post book reviews! Who knew!

Her cellphone rang just as she was about to head to the bathroom for that shower, and she looked down at the caller ID, already rolling her eyes. She didn't know why she didn't just put the damn thing on silent; the only people who ever called were her own phone company telling her about promotions or just plain spam—

She paused with a foot inside the bathroom, her shirt half-hanging onto her arm.

Janet, the caller ID read.

Joanne didn't want to answer. She even considered not answering for a few seconds, just enough that maybe Janet would give up and hang up before she had to come to a decision—but of course Janet persevered.

Joanne couldn't not answer.

"Janet!" she exclaimed, infusing her voice with enough cheer to knock a clown's socks off. "So nice to hear from you! It's been, what, a whole week since I've seen you? How have you been?"

"You moved to another state?" Janet asked, clearly too baffled still to have become properly furious about it.

Joanne shrugged, letting her shirt drop to the floor. She shut the bathroom door behind her. "I told you I would. Didn't I? I probably did. Or if I didn't, there was probably a reason. There was probably a reason, Janet, if I might have forgotten—or perhaps purposefully—didn't tell you about the fact that I was moving, though what I do remember was leaving a note, and on the note asking you not to call me. Remember that?"

"You can't just move to another state out of the blue," Janet cut in, clearly not having heard a single word Joanne had just said. She was much closer to the fury now than she had been before. "Mom says you're on the West Cost, but that's impossible. Look, if you're just over at Kath's and playing a prank—"

"It's not a prank and I haven't spoken to Kath in months," Joanne said with a roll of her eyes. "Look, I know you're angry, and maybe I should have left something more than a note—"

"You can't be on the West Cost."

"All right, if you think so."

"Joanne," her older sister said, patience audibly thin, "come back home. What on Earth are you doing?"

"I'm doing just fine!" Joanne exclaimed instead of telling her that she didn't know, that she had no idea, that she just couldn't stay where she had been anymore. That she woke up one day and realized that she was going to die if she stayed put where she had always been, in her parents' house, in her comfortable life; that she was going to wither where she stood.

"And I'm late to a thing, actually," she added, even though she wasn't, because she didn't want to talk to Janet anymore. She wanted Janet not to have called, to have left her in her new life. "So, I have to go! See you!"

"Joanne don't you dare—"

She hung up, then turned off her phone, just in case Janet called again. She chucked off her shorts and her underwear, turned on the shower, and stepped under the too-hot spray as if the water were going to wash that conversation away.

Chapter Two

Beatriz sat in front of her brother in the upscale restaurant he had chosen for their rendezvous and felt very thankful, not for the first time, that her natural expression was a blank, stoic face.

"—and you know how Julie is with the kids; I couldn't even get them out of the pool before she was attacking them with more sunscreen—"

She nodded blandly and speared another piece of salmon with her fork. Beau looked exactly like her in appearance (though she would allow, if pressed, that he was slightly taller) but in personality he was the complete opposite. She dealt with the stifled, awkward atmosphere between them by keeping quiet and letting him talk; he, in turn, talked about anything and everything that crossed his mind.

She was now aware of how many freckles his son had, three separate fights he had with his wife, which coworker had said what during the last two meetings he had at the hospital he worked at, and exactly which breeds of dog his daughter was planning on competitively breeding when she was older.

"—king of the jungle, which was when I told him that we would absolutely not get him a monkey—"

Bea scrutinized the salmon on her fork while trying to still look like she was paying utmost attention. It didn't taste any different than the salmon she had bought at the supermarket last week. What was it, exactly, that made it about five times more expensive?

"—and then the dog started screaming and I swear I heard him actually say a word—"

Bea narrowed her eyes. She would never come to places like this if her brother didn't drag her here whenever he was in town. If she had the money he had, she would go to much better places.

"—and then I told her, Beatriz, well... I had no idea what to tell her."

Her gaze snapped back to her brother. She mentally backtracked through the conversation to try and see what he had been saying, and when her brain showed her that piece of information, it was an effort not to let her expressionless face turn sour.

"I don't really discuss that type of thing with you," she said, offering him an explanation.

"Yes," he agreed in that easy way people agreed with you when they wanted something out of you. He took a sip of his wine. "But, speaking of discussing about it... how is your love life? I don't remember you mentioning having anyone at all since—God, since med school."

"I haven't had anything to speak about since med school," she informed him, eating another forkful of her salmon. "As you know."

He pursed his lips. "Well. Why?"

She glared at him. "I don't want to talk about this kind of thing. I don't understand why you're bringing it up. Usually during these meetings, we discuss your wife and your children and your work and leave very content."

She didn't like him changing their routine, stifled and uncomfortable as it was.

"I worry about you," he told her, lowering his glass of wine back to the table. She could tell by his expression that he was genuine, but it still chafed at

14

her; they were not close at all, aside from their having lunch now and then, when he came home from being the fanciest, richest hospital owner in the world to visit his general practitioner of a sister.

"You don't need to worry about me," she told him evenly.

"You haven't had anyone in years. I'm married with children and I'm only two years older…"

"Congratulations," she told him dryly.

He sent her a sour look.

"I am busy with work," she told him, as she always told herself when this sort of subject was raised. "I have the clinic to worry about and patients to occupy my time, and do not feel wanting of a relationship of any kind. Are you telling me that you thought I was doing better when I was dating—what was his name? Clark? That was a disaster I do not want to repeat, either way."

"Clark just wasn't the right man for you!" he exclaimed. "If you search for the right person…"

"I don't want to search," she told him frankly. "I am not interested."

Truthfully, the thought of having to go through the tribulations of getting to know a man, then the whole mess of dating, and then having to spend her entire life with a man; it didn't appeal to her at all.

It never occurred to her to ponder on why—except for once, when she was twelve, after which she buried those feelings very deep indeed.

"And the practice… I keep telling you that you can find work somewhere better than that," Beau told her frankly, a line between his brows.

"I'm happy," she told him firmly, and very graciously did not make a point of pointing out all the awful parts of his life, as he surely would do to her if she gave him as many details as he foisted onto her.

He sighed, but let it go. He moved on to other things and she drooped with relief, glad that it was done, at least for now. He would be in town for a couple of months this time, sorting something or other with a friend who needed his help, and she knew this was not the last she would hear of this.

***

Bea arrived at the clinic a bit later than usual, but no one would bat an eye, since everyone knew her brother sometimes liked to whisk her away to subpar rich lunches when he was in town. She went straight to her office, nodding at Robert at the reception.

"—so, what did he make you eat today?" Robert asked her with a grin before she could make her escape.

She paused and turned to him. Robert was a nice man, and she didn't mind lingering by to chat for a bit.

"Just a nice salmon dish," she told him. "It was very good, though I wouldn't have paid so much for it."

"Your brother just loves shoving in your face how successful he is," Robert said with an eye roll. "Don't let him intimidate you."

"He doesn't intimidate me," Bea said, amused that Robert would think so. "I'm happy he's successful."

"You're too kind," Robert said with a smile, propping his cheek up with a hand. "So. Um. Aside from adequate salmon, how was your lunch?"

"Adequate," she told him. "Did anyone leave any messages for me?"

"No," he told her, seemingly disappointed for some reason. "But the day is young, they still might. Speaking of the day being young... I remember the other day you mentioning you went to salsa lessons on Wednesday nights...?"

Bea grimaced before she could help it, and Robert raised his eyebrows in curiosity.

"An attempt to exercise while escaping the gym," she told him, pronouncing gym like one would pronounce grievous bodily harm. "But it's not really my favorite thing."

She thought she would love it in other circumstances, but she definitely didn't in circumstances that made several strange men hold her close to them for nearly two hours. She knew it was just dancing, it was just fun, she needed to learn to relax, to unwind, that was what the classes were for, and she tried every week—and every week the first man put his hand on her waist and her body locked up.

She wouldn't mind dancing the gentleman's steps, dancing with other women, if only she didn't know she wouldn't be mocked for it.

"I guess I had thought about going, too..." Robert said, sounding a bit embarrassed. "I'm also not too fond of the gym," he said, the way someone would say *cockroaches in my pillowcase*, "but if you don't like it, then I guess I wouldn't either."

"You might," Bea said with a shrug. "But I think you're better off going to the gym after all, Robert. You told me you have a yearly subscription, so—"

"No, don't remind me of that!"

"—you should at least go to the gym until the year is done," she continued.

He sighed. "You're right. I don't have the time, anyway; I have to write. I finished another chapter yesterday, by the way!"

"Congrats," she said, and was glad to see the conversation was over; his book was always the last thing Robert ever brought up before making to go back to work.

He went back to his computer and she walked on to her office, which was small but tidy and entirely hers, and for that, entirely perfect. She sat down behind her desk and thought about salsa after all, and about her conversation with her brother, and for some reason it all brought to her mind the image of Joanne Parker, the new woman in the class.

She had seemed bashful at first, but when the class started, she had shone brighter than anyone. She had laughed any time anyone had twirled around the room, her mess of curls flying around her red face. She looked well; flushed with life.

Bea looked down at her own hands. Joanne had been the opposite of her.

I really wouldn't mind, she thought, thinking about Joanne, *getting to dance with her instead*.

***

Salsa again was only a few days later, and something about Joanne had firmed the thought in her mind: she would speak to the teachers and ask if she couldn't learn the other steps after all. A part of her still recoiled from putting herself so much at the center of attention, but she wanted to be like Joanne had been: so light, so happy.

Maybe, just maybe, Joanne herself would be okay with dancing with her.

She arrived early enough that the room was mostly empty; as it were, most people tended to arrive late, especially the couples. Bea was glad for it, since it would allow her some privacy when speaking to the teachers. She headed straight for them—they were both standing at the front of the class and chatting quietly to each other.

"Vivian, Marcus," she greeted them easily. They turned and nodded at her but didn't pause in their conversation. She cleared her throat and they blinked, turning to her. "Sorry for interrupting your conversation. I will be just a minute. I was wondering if it'd be all right for me to start learning the gentleman's steps instead. I think I'd do much better with them."

"It's okay if you want to learn them, but you need to finish learning what you started or you'll just confuse yourself," Vivian said, a line between her brows. "Me and Marcus know all the steps and we can switch when we want, but that takes a lot of practice. You can't just stop in the middle and start again..."

"Besides, come on, a pretty woman like you wanting to learn the guy's steps?" Marcus asked, playful. "Don't you want to be twirled around the room? The lady's part is always more fun, you know."

"It's the short hair, she looks like a guy!" one of the other students piped up, not mocking as much as simply joking.

Bea turned to him with a dry look on her face. He immediately realized he should not be joking with people he didn't know and made an apologetic sort of face at her.

"You need to finish what you started now," Vivian said, more firmly. "Maybe you can start again next semester at the first module to switch the steps instead of moving forward, if you want, but if you do it now…"

"Well, it isn't like she isn't tall enough to pass for a guy," a woman piped up. The comment itself wouldn't raise eyebrows, but her tone of voice made Bea wonder if it wouldn't have been better to just stop coming after all.

"Dude, we're not learning to dance competitively or anything like that," another voice started, cheerful and nearly threatening with it, as if they were ready to turn this into an actual fight if you wanted. "I mean, is anyone going to die if Bea stumbles on some steps sometimes? We're pretty much beginners anyway, so will it really make a difference if she switches now instead of next semester or whatever?"

There was a pause.

Bea turned around.

Joanne was standing right beside her, hands on her waist and a grin on her face like she knew she had won. It was stupid, really; this was just salsa class, not anything important. People's jokes didn't matter and it wouldn't be the end of the world if Bea stopped coming.

But Joanne hadn't joked. She hadn't shrugged or stayed quiet or thought it weird.

"I guess it won't make that much of a difference in the long term," Marcus admitted.

"Then that's that," Joanne said easily, shrugging like she was tossing the subject away.

"Thank you," Bea said, honestly and simply.

Joanne blinked at her and slowly a blush rose to her face, coloring it pink.

"It's nothing," she said, seemingly embarrassed. "I mean, being honest, I'd rather dance with another woman than with a man I don't know, so…"

"That's what I thought, too," Bea said. "I'm glad you're okay with it. I wasn't sure any women would want to dance with me."

"Of course they will dance with you," Vivian said sharply. "Actually, why don't you start the first dance with Joanne? She's just starting as well, so you two should be at about the same level. Marcus, music."

"All right, all right," her husband said easily.

The music started. People started pairing up around the room. Bea looked at Joanne and felt suddenly bashful herself, and hoped she wasn't blushing. She had no reason to blush. Why was she even afraid she would be doing it? She stepped forward and reached out for the other woman, palm up. Joanne set her hand in hers.

Bea was a fast learner. She had been watching the men since the first day, aside from dancing with them, and knew more or less what to do.

She clasped Joanne's hand in hers and twirled her, careful with what she was doing but wanting to

make it look easy. She smiled when the other woman
let out a pearl of surprised, delighted laughter.

Chapter Three

Thursday morning, Joanne was nearly skipping her steps as she made her way to the nearest shopping mall. She felt like she was swimming in endorphins, so happy and cheerful she felt; yesterday had been the best salsa class she had ever had, a statement she thought with conviction even though it had only been the second one ever.

Bea had been an amazing dancer. Joanne wished she could dance all the songs with her, even though the teachers insisted that unmatched people switch partners every song.

As she walked along the streets and entered the small mall, she thought about how Bea had been tall, but hadn't towered over her like the men had; how she had held her, careful like Joanne was made of glass, the touch of her skin smooth and rough at the same time the way only the hands of someone who was constantly washing them felt; how it hadn't felt awkward at all to be so close, to be held against her body or by the hands, to have Bea catch her after twirls and spin her around again...

Joanne blinked and saw she was inside the mall and all the way into the food court and hadn't even realized it, so distracted she had been thinking about B—about dancing. She looked around, trying to spot anything interesting to eat.

Maybe she wouldn't have seen Bea if she hadn't been looking around with wide eyes trying to spot anything more interesting than pasta or hamburgers, but as it was, there was no way she could have missed her: Bea was standing right in front of one of those maps to the mall with a small bag in one hand and her chin in the other.

"Bea!" Joanne exclaimed, delighted.

The woman turned around distractedly, like she had heard her name but didn't believe anyone was really calling her. Her dark eyes widened she caught sight of Joanne power-walking her way to her.

"Joanne," she said.

"What's up?" Joanne asked. "I thought nicely employed people would be working right now."

"It's Saturday," Bea pointed out with a smile. "Are you here on an errand?"

"Nah, just looking for a coffee shop." Joanne was struck by an idea, that her mouth ran with before she could stop it. "Do you want to come with me? If you're not too busy."

Bea blinked at her in surprise. Joanne felt her face flush but resisted the urge to look away and deflect and kept her eyes firmly on Bea, waiting for her answer.

"Of course," Bea said at last, then winced. "I mean—of course, let's have some coffee. I just passed by to buy some new socks, and that's done."

"All right," Joanne said, too relieved and thankful for what should just be a possible friend accepting to hang out with her. "Do you know any coffee shops around? I know I invited you, but I have no idea."

Bea laughed—a quiet, small laugh, like she wasn't used to doing it—and Joanne felt something in her chest squeeze her heart.

***

Bea led her to a coffee shop nearby, both of them walking in silence. She was clearly familiar with the place, and it made Joanne smile, because it looked like the sort of place she would like: plain, simple, and mostly empty. She led Joanne to a specific table, one in the corner but away from both the counter and the windows and gestured for Joanne to sit.

"I'll get our order," she said. "What do you want? Just coffee?"

Joanne's eyebrows furrowed over her eyes. "Wait. I invited you. I'll order for us."

"I'm nicely employed," Bea countered with an amused smile. "Thank you, but let it be my treat."

Joanne geared up to argue. She didn't need charity. She wasn't stupid, she had moved here with savings, she could afford some coffee—but something about Bea's expression stopped her. The woman looked amused, yes, but also uncertain, like she wasn't sure what she was doing but really wanted to do it. And, a part of Joanne for some reason felt tickled pink at the thought of Bea treating her like this.

"All right," she said softly. "Um. Just black coffee is good for me." A line appeared between Bea's brows. "... and a cookie if they have it?"

"Okay," Bea said, expression clearing up. "I'll probably get the same for me. I'll be right back."

She returned a few minutes later with a tray.

"Thanks," Joanne said. "Next time it'll be on me."

Bea smiled, which dissipated any anxiety Joanne could have felt about implying they would hang out again. Joanne brought her cup to her lips and took a sip, blowing on the steam to try and cool it a bit.

"You're unemployed, then?" Bea asked quietly, not looking up from her own coffee as she stirred in some sugar. "In what field do you work?"

Joanne shrugged. "Many things. I used to work as a cashier slash accountant slash secretary for my mom's shop, doing some freelance everything on the side. Editing, revising, web design, beta reading and proof reading. All kind of informal, though, all to friends and friends of friends. I actually have a course on editing under my belt now though, so I was hoping to find something related to it. So if you need anyone to, I don't know, revise your e-mails before you send them, hit me up," she said, sending Bea a grin.

"I'll keep it in mind. I don't think I could handle that," Bea admitted, still stirring sugar into her coffee. "Being a freelancer, that is, not having much stability or security. You need to have a lot of discipline, I suppose."

"Oh, yeah," Joanne said seriously. "Discipline. That's my middle name." She smiled when Bea laughed. "What do you do, then? Let's see if I was right."

Bea lifted one eyebrow. "I'm a doctor."

"Yes!" Joanne exclaimed, taking one victorious bite of her cookie. "I'd pegged you for a lawyer or a doctor since the first time I saw you," she explained to Bea's confused face. "You have that air about you, calm competence. Is it a family business? It usually is."

Bea winced. "It is."

"You don't have to talk about it if you don't want to," Joanne said quietly, sensing a change in mood.

"It's okay." She waved a dismissive hand. "My brother is also a doctor and owns a hospital, though neither of our parents works in the field. It's just—well, I'm a GP, which is what I want for myself, but my brother is a surgeon who owns a hospital, so..."

"The parents love bringing it up, I imagine," Joanne said.

"They are very fond of this subject, yes," she said dryly, then grew quiet. She looked down at her super-sugared coffee. "They are very... disappointed, I suppose. All of them. I am not really a model daughter, or sister."

"You're a doctor," Joanne said, baffled. "What's not to be proud about?"

Bea shrugged. "I'm nearly forty and have never married, don't have any children, am just a GP. And it's not like I go travelling around the world or, I don't know, breed corgis or grow orchids or anything like that. I am, sadly enough, a very boring person with a very average life."

"That's a load of bullshit," Joanne said plainly, chewing on the last of her cookie.

Bea looked up at her, surprised at her candid tone.

"You're an amazing salsa dancer, for one," Joanne said with a grin.

It brought a smile to Bea's face, which was what she had been gunning for.

"Fuck your brother and your parents, honestly," she continued. "You're a doctor, what's to complain about that? I bet your brother gave them grandkids, even if you haven't." Bea lifted two fingers and Joanne snorted. "See? My parents at least can complain about me never going to college and moving out to the other side of the country out of nowhere!"

"Oh?" Bea said, interest and curiosity packed in a small word.

Joanne shrugged; she didn't want to talk about it—but she did, or else she wouldn't have brought it up. She decided to not expand much on things as a compromise.

"I wanted to help them at the shop instead of getting into thousands of debt straight after high school," Joanne said with a shrug. "It's not my fault Mom decided to close the shop out of nowhere. And then the years passed and I just… I don't know." She sighed. "I just needed to go away. I needed to leave, to be apart from everything and everyone, to go somewhere new. So here I am."

"You just… moved?" Bea asked.

"Yep," Joanne said. "With no job and no plan, though with a lot of savings, so it's not like I'm going to starve."

"That's very brave," Bea said quietly.

Joanne felt something that had been tied into knots in her chest suddenly smooth out, defensiveness she hadn't even noticed she was ready to unleash turning into relief. She had been expecting disapproval or even dismissiveness, but not to be called brave.

"I'm glad you think so," Joanne said, just as quiet.

They looked at each other, Joanne's hazel eyes on Bea's dark brown ones, and didn't say anything. Their hands were close on top of the table, close enough that either could stretch it forward and touch the other. But they didn't, and after a moment Joanne cracked a joke about Bea being a doctor and still drinking coffee with enough sugar to kill a man, and Bea smiled and said something about knowing better.

They spent another hour like this, both hoping the other would mention a phone or another meetup, but neither did, and they went home not knowing how they felt.

***

Joanne laid down on Carla's bed and played word games on her phone while Carla sat on her computer chair and did something important looking with some files. She was dressed up and ready to leave; Carla was just killing time doing something work-related until one of the others texted her saying they were ready and she could go pick them up and drive everyone to the show.

"It's not really a show," Carla said. "It's just another very small performance at a bar. I keep telling Jacob that if he tells everybody that it's a show, then people will think it's something more than it is and be disappointed when they arrive!"

"Maybe people will demand that the bar let you have an actual show, then," Joanne said with a grin.

"Maybe I'll break up with Jacob and get back with Tiana, who was a much better band manager," Carla muttered.

Joanne's mouth fell open. "Oh—you're—you were with—um."

Carla slowly turned around on her chair to look at her, both of her eyebrows up. "What?"

"You dated a woman?" Joanne asked, a red flush rising to her cheeks.

29

"Wait, you're straight?" Carla asked, baffled.

"What? Yes! Why would you think I'm not?" Joanne asked, lifting a hand to her burning cheek. "I didn't—I never..."

"Are you in the closet? You can tell me, you know," Carla said, sympathetic.

"I'm not in the closet," Joanne retorted, shaking her head sharply—then thought of Bea and went really quiet.

"Aren't you?" Carla asked, narrowing her eyes.

"No!" Joanne denied, shaking her head and trying to dislodge her own stupid thoughts. "I'm not you, living your best life with your band and your international trips and your guitarist boyfriend."

"Ahem," Carla said, though she didn't sound convinced. "You could be like me, you know. Go live your best life. Visit Peru. Learn how to play the drums. Sleep with a woman."

Joanne sent her a sour look, then went back to her game, on which she resolutely focused.

Carla laughed. "I'm just joking with you! It's none of my business who you want to sleep with or not. I just thought you were gay, that's all. Just like you thought I was straight. Honestly, the nerve. Do I look straight?"

Joanne looked up. Carla had a blue strand in her hair, was wearing a top with a mesh shirt under it, and Joanne was pretty sure that she was wearing rainbow-colored striped socks under the long skirt.

"No," Joanne admitted.

Carla laughed.

Chapter Four

Bea would be lying if she said that she hadn't been looking forward to salsa class all week long, or that she hadn't spent more time in front of the mirror trying to figure out what to wear than she had spent the rest of her life all put together. She didn't quite know why, but she felt nervous. Not apprehensive, just... she didn't know how to describe it.

She gave herself one last look before leaving. It wouldn't do to keep worrying at her hair like a schoolgirl with a crush.

***

She arrived before Joanne did, a fact which made her sad. She had wanted to chat with the woman before class started. She stayed in her spot, quiet, until the room filled and mostly checked her phone. She really didn't know anyone else, and people who had already made friends were all talking to each other. She was glad to see Joanne once she walked in, but it was too late for them to talk.

Joanne still made her way to her, a fact which brought a smile to Bea's face.

"Hello. You're a bit late," Bea said.

"You noticed?" Joanne asked with a smile.

"I had wanted to ask you about the show you went to, but the class is about to start," Bea said sadly, turning to look pointedly at the teachers as they turned on the music and urged people to get into positions.

"We can talk while we dance," Joanne told her, reaching out with a hand and a smile.

Bea caught the hand automatically, for all that she felt a bit surprised—she forgot, for a moment, that she could do this now, hold Joanne's hand and dance with her instead of bracing herself to have Jared's or Paul's or Pedro's hands on her. Joanne immediately fit her body against hers and Bea suppressed a blush.

They started to move, Bea counting the steps carefully—forwards with left, back. Backwards with right, back—while Joanne easily followed her lead and looked amused besides.

"You always have such a look of concentration on your face," she said.

"I am concentrating on dancing," Bea pointed out.

"What about letting go and feeling the rhythm?"

Bea couldn't suppress the blush anymore. She fit her fingers to the sweet curves of Joanne's waist and about swallowed her tongue, feeling all of 12 and rather like someone stuffed the sun into her face.

"I don't want to step on your foot," she admitted quietly.

"I'll forgive you," Joanne said.

When Bea looked up from their feet and at Joanne's face, Joanne was very close, looking straight at her, and had a pink flush to her face.

"Nice blush," Bea said somewhat awkwardly. "What brand is it?"

The color darkened. "Um. I don't really wear make-up."

"Oh."

She was just really, actually blushing.

"Are you girls having a tea party in the middle of class? Back to dancing!" Vivian, the teacher, called out, half amused, half annoyed. "And stop looking at your feet, Beatriz!"

Bea winced and tried not to look down, and realized she would have to dance while looking at Joanne, whose face was a palm away from hers.

"I believe in you. You can do it without looking at your feet," the woman said, encouraging and finding the situation far too funny.

"Next time we go out for coffee, I'm buying the whole establishment and making you pay," Bea muttered.

Joanne laughed, and managed to convince the teacher to let them dance another song together.

***

When the doorbell rang, Bea felt her spine straighten up even more, her hands closing in fists. She stopped what she was doing—putting the last touches on a half-hearted salad—and made her way to the door. Beau was on the other side, carrying three boxes of pizza like they were 20 years younger and hadn't eaten in a full week. She recognized the brand—from that fancy place four blocks away that she never went to because they were too expensive and didn't even have breadsticks.

"Bea, hi," he said, walking in. "I didn't know what flavors you liked so I brought a bunch, I hope something here is to your taste. You can keep the leftovers, too."

"Thank you," she said evenly, instead of telling him she didn't mind any type of pizza, much less enough to have three boxes for leftovers in her fridge.

33

He set the boxes down on her coffee table and sat down on the couch. She sat opposite him on the other side of the couch.

"How have you been?" she asked before he could do the same.

"Just fine," he said smoothly. "I hope you've been fine as well."

"Yes."

They were quiet for a moment.

"Shall I go get us some plates?" she asked, standing up again.

"Wait," he said, catching her wrist and stopping her from going. "I'm not really hungry… I bet you're not too, it's barely five yet. Just sit down. Can we talk?"

Bea swallowed down apprehension and sat back down. She wished, suddenly and fervently, that she had stayed at the clinic, chatting with Robert and waiting for the patients as they arrived for their consults. She wanted to practice salsa in her closed office and to stay over after hours to clean things up and to talk to the nurses.

"All right."

"You know I worry about you," he said carefully, as if he knew that this phrase was going to make her side-eye whatever he could say next, "especially when it comes to your…well, the romance area of your life. You've always been an awkward kid, Bea—"

"I'm thirty-nine years old," she told him blandly.

"—and I'm afraid for you," he continued softly, as if she hadn't interrupted. "I don't want you to spend your life alone."

Bea opened her mouth then closed it again. She had been ready to tell him the usual: that she had work, that she was busy, that she didn't think of it. But the truth was that she didn't want to spend her days alone, either. And she was so alone, every day. She had Robert and the nurses and it wasn't enough—they weren't her friends.

"I'm not unhappy, Beau," she told him.

"I have a friend," he said carefully.

"Beau," she said, giving an explosive sigh.

"Hear me out! I have a friend and he'll be wonderful for you! He's not a doctor, but he's a nurse and he knows how the job is, he's understanding of the odd hours we have to pull sometimes, he's tall and green-eyed and he laughs at even the jokes I make, and you know my jokes are worse than yours. His name is Antonio. Won't you give him a chance?"

"I'm not twelve, Beau," Bea growled. "I don't need you setting up dates for me as if I can't do anything by myself."

"I'm not saying you can't, I'm just saying...he's a good guy," he said. "What's the harm in it? Just go have some coffee with him this Saturday just to meet him. It's just coffee, it doesn't have to last more than half an hour, and if you hate him you don't have to ever see him again. How about it?"

Bea wasn't going to give in. She didn't want to give in. But she looked at her brother and felt herself unable to say no, if not for his pleading, worried face, then because she suddenly was afraid that she really couldn't do anything by herself, that maybe these past years of solitude were her fault after all, inept woman that she was.

"I do not like you doing this," she hissed, reaching for one of the pizza boxes. "You will not do this again. Understood?"

"So, you'll meet him?" he asked, relieved.

"I'll meet him, and will most definitely not like him," she muttered.

***

They met in front of the café. Antonio was indeed a tall man—taller than her, which did not endear him to her. His hair was brown and so was his face, and they contrasted prettily with his green eyes, though for some reason she found herself not finding him all that beautiful. The eyes were too light, the hair not curled enough, she caught herself thinking, then wasn't sure what exactly she was comparing him to.

"It's nice to meet you," he said, smiling sweetly at her. "You can get anything you want, it's my treat. Where do you want to sit?"

"Anywhere is fine," she said awkwardly, wary of choosing precisely the place he would hate the most. "And I can pay for my own coffee, it's fine."

"Let me treat you," he said, leading her toward a table near the windows. "I want to be a gentleman, you know?" He smiled as if sharing an in-joke and pulled her chair back for her.

She instantly hated it.

She didn't want him pulling her chair back for her, or paying for her, or being a gentleman, or being taller than her. But she couldn't just walk out right now, so she sat down and smiled back at him as much as she could and kindly asked him for a black coffee and nothing else, no, nothing else, no sandwich, no brownie, nothing, thanks.

She sat in silence until he came back with a tray. He had brought her a brownie after all, though he set it in the middle of the table and said it was for him, for when he was done with his pastry.

"So… Beau tells me you're a doctor, too?" he asked into the silence.

"Yes," she said. "And you're a nurse, he said."

"Yeah, it's a family thing, my two sisters and my father are all nurses too. I guess it's a family thing for you guys too?"

"Sort of," she said, and didn't elaborate.

They lapsed into silence. Antonio sweetened his coffee and so did she, adding enough packs that Joanne would have definitely poked her about it by now. He just eyed her coffee and grimaced a bit.

Bea drank her coffee and tried to find something to talk about.

"Where did you meet my brother?" she settled on.

"Oh, we were college roommates!" he said brightly. "I was actually surprised I'd never met you before, he's told me so much about you."

"Has he," she said.

"All good things!" Antonio rushed to reassure her, a look in his face like he was just figuring out that being college buddies with her older brother was not the way into her heart. "Um, I mean, he didn't speak that much—you know how he is. Tight-lipped. So… what are your hobbies?"

She saw that desperate question for what it was. She wanted the easy conversation she had had with Joanne, the way the other woman had laughed, had blushed, had accepted that Bea pay for her coffee. Would she had let Bea pull her chair back for her?

Why was she thinking about Joanne right now? She shouldn't be thinking about Joanne. She should be thinking about her date with Antonio.

But the truth was, Bea wished she were on a date with Joanne instead.

"Bea, are you all right?" Antonio asked. "You just went pale all of a sudden. Was it the coffee, or…?"

"No, no, I'm fine," she managed to choke out, lifting her cup back to her face so she could hide behind it.

She didn't wish she were on a date with Joanne instead. She couldn't. She wasn't—she had never—but she did. She wanted Joanne here, with her wild brown curls and her hazel eyes, with whom Bea could dance, holding her body close, feeling her soft skin, shorter than her and beautiful, so beautiful. She wanted Joanne to joke, to grin, to share stories about her life.

"Are you sure you're okay?" Antonio asked, worried.

"I'm just fine," Bea said, covering her face with both her hands.

Out of all the reasons to never have a boyfriend, she thought to herself, *I didn't see this one coming.*

Chapter Five

Joanne shoved her leg into the colorful legging she had bought yesterday and had been really looking forward to wearing today for salsa class and tried not to trip on her own feet and fall to the floor.

"No, I hadn't found a job yet," she said, teeth gritted.

"If you had stayed, you could have kept on with the clients you had here," her sister said reproachfully, not even trying not to spark a fight even though it was the first time in a few weeks that Joanne actually answered the phone to talk to her. "I know you only had a couple of people paying you and it wouldn't be enough to keep up rent by yourself, but at least it was something—"

"It was enough for me to save money to pay rent alone now, so I'm not complaining," Joanne told her sweetly. "And it's not my fault that neither George nor Cora wanted to give up our face-to-face meetings, even though we could totally do that through video-calls. But it's fine. I'll find a job at a publishing press or something—"

"Which you've just told me is going nowhere fast," Janet interrupted dryly.

"I will hang up on you," Joanne told her. "I will hang up on you and never answer again. Is that what you want?"

"I want you to stop being so childish," her sister snapped. Joanne bit back too-harsh words and heard Janet breathing out a tired sigh. "Look," she said. "I'm sorry, all right? I'm just—I just don't understand why you left us."

"I know you don't," Joanne muttered, and the truth was that she didn't either, really.

They were both quiet for a moment. Joanne tugged up her pants and went searching for a sports bra. She needed to leave soon, or she'd be late for class. She was still excited to go, even with Janet's call putting a damper on her spirits. They were learning some more complicated steps now, the names of which she could never really remember—she knew the comb, the in-and-out, and not much else— and she felt like moving. She'd like to practice at home, but she had no one to practice with...

"Let me visit," Janet said suddenly. "Don't interrupt me, just—let me visit you. Just to see that you're okay, that you're actually living somewhere good, that everything's all right. And I want to talk to you in person, not through the phone. Let me visit for a weekend a couple of weeks from now."

Joanne wanted her to come.

The wish hit her like a punch to the chest and she abruptly sat down on her bed. She wanted to see her big sister, the chasm between them suddenly bigger than she could deal with, Janet and their parents on the other side of the county while she was here doing god-knows-what, having moved for no reason she could understand. Joanne stared at the wall, biting her bottom lip hard enough to hurt.

She missed them. But she thought, then and there, that Janet was cruel, too.

"I asked you for space," Joanne said, voice quiet. "I told you I needed to be away for some time. Why do you ask me something like that? Why are you so desperate to see me?"

Janet was quiet. Joanne's eyebrows lowered over her eyes, which narrowed.

"Janet?" she asked. "Why are you desperate to see me?"

"If you don't want me to come, fine," Janet said instead of answering. "But I want to see my little sister. Why is that such an awful mystery to you?"

"Is something actually going on?" Joanne asked, standing up as if that would do anything; her sister wasn't here and couldn't see her.

"No," Janet lied. "Can I visit?"

"No," Joanne said.

"All right. See you later."

Without another word, Janet hung up. Joanne stood in the middle of her messy, barely furnished bedroom and stared at her phone, trying to understand what on Earth was up with her sister.

***

It was a relief to have to go to class, to have a responsibility that meant she had to leave the house and stop thinking about her sister. Fortunately, the studio wasn't too far from her place and she arrived slightly early, just enough that the teachers couldn't make faces at her and then point at the clock. She crept in slowly, eyes roaming the room, as she set her purse down on the floor and started pulling her hair up into a bun.

She didn't find Bea.

Disappointment curdled in her chest. She lowered her arms, letting her hair fall wild again, and looked around again: Bea wasn't in her usual place, by the back of the room and on her phone; she wasn't talking to the teachers or anything else; the door to the bathroom was open and there was no one there; her purse wasn't on the floor, so she wasn't anywhere either.

Bea wasn't the sort of person who was ever late. Still, life was a box of surprises, right? Joanne tried to tell herself that maybe Bea was about to show up, and then would tell her why exactly she wasn't on time—maybe a patient had a problem more complicated than she had expected, maybe there was traffic, who knew?

But the minutes passed until the teachers went on to turn on the music and ask people to get into positions, and Bea still didn't show up.

Joanne felt her excitement disappear like a candle being blown out. She smiled awkwardly at the man who approached her and took her hand—it was Hiroshi, a perfectly nice guy with whom she had danced many times before. Right now though, she surprised herself with how much she didn't want him to touch her. She wanted to dance with Bea.

I was looking forward to seeing Beatriz, she noticed in a snap, looking up at the man in front of her, *and not to coming to class*.

She stumbled as she danced, forcing the man to compensate for her heavy, awkward weight, but she wasn't paying attention to him or to the music. Her eyes unfocused as she thought about Bea, about where she could be, why she wasn't here—and about the fact that she had no way to ask, because she didn't have Bea's number.

She had no way to contact her, no way to reach Bea if Bea or she stopped coming to class.

She had to get Bea's number somehow.

She looked at Vivian. She was dancing with one of the men and correcting his steps as they moved. Joanne could talk to her after class. She probably had Bea's number and could be convinced to pass it on to Joanne, and then Joanne would be able to reach Bea.

***

"Hey," Joanne greeted, drawing out the vowel. "How are you doing? I hope I'm not interrupting?"

Vivian turned to her, though her hands didn't stop putting everything away into her bag: her coat, her water bottle, a few notebooks.

"No. Do you need something?"

"I saw that Bea didn't come today," Joanne started. "I wanted to ask her what's wrong because she's my friend, but I realized I don't have her number. Can you give it to me?"

Vivian grimaced. "Look, I know that you're friends, but I can't do that. If anything happens, I don't want Bea coming to me and complaining. You just need to get her number from her."

"Nothing is going to happen," Jo argued. "I just want to make sure she's all right."

"Sorry," Vivian said with a shrug.

Joanne bit her lip and thought. She should have told her that she already had the number and lost it for some reason. How would she convince her now?

"If you have her number," Joanne said slowly, "could you text her with my number and ask that she call me?"

Vivian narrowed her eyes, then shrugged. "All right, I don't see why not, if you're giving me permission to give her your number. I'll tell her you're asking after her. Don't ask me to give out personal details of my students again, all right? I don't care if Bea's house is on fire, I still won't give you the address."

"All right!" Joanne said, grinning with success.

***

Joanne was late. She rushed to the bar and craned her neck to see over the throng of people, trying to spot her face. She brightened when she did and ran to them, throwing herself into the seat beside Carla, knocking their shoulders together painfully.

"Ouch! First you're late, then you cause me bodily harm?" Carla asked, rubbing at her shoulder.

"It's your punishment for telling me we were meeting at the wrong bar," Joanne said easily, snagging the drink Carla had in front of her and taking a sip. It was nice; passion fruit and vodka.

"Give me that, you thieving fiend!" Carla exclaimed, stealing it back.

"That's mine," Jacob said, amused. He had an arm around Carla's shoulder and another around Bob, who was already three times drunker than everyone else and more lying on his seat than sitting on it. "Hey, Joanne. What do you want? Bob is paying the first round for everyone."

"Awesome," Joanne said with a grin. "Just a beer for now, I don't want to abuse the poor man's wallet."

"Better his wallet than mine," another voice piped up. Joanne turned: it was Julien who was leaning against Laura, both of them with flushes high in their faces and grinning at her with identical smiles. "I need to save money for our trip, after all!"

Joanne felt her entire being brighten. "Have you guys settled where you're going?"

"The Iguassu Falls in Brazil and then, Argentina!" Carla yelled with joy, throwing her drink to the sky. The others—Jacob, Bob, Julien, and Laura, all of them Joanne's new friends—raised their drinks for a toast. "Cheers!"

"We're not sure when we're going, but it'll be soon," Jacob said with bright eyes. "We've all been saving money for so long, none of us want to wait."

"When are you guys thinking, broadly?" she asked. "The end of the year?"

"Yeah, around December maybe," Carla told her with a grin. "It's June, so we'll still have some time, but half a year is short enough that we can bear it."

"Wow," Joanne said, wistful and filled with longing, "you guys are really living the life I wish I was."

Chapter Six

Bea watched as her brother took the tray out of the oven with a flourish. He turned to her with a smug grin, brandishing the admittedly beautiful dish so she could see it: on a dark blue dish, an artful mess of eggplant, onions, red and yellow bell peppers, and potatoes sat. It smelled amazing.

Bea did not like eggplant. She was not sure if her brother had forgotten about it or if this was another way for him to annoy her.

"Beautiful," she told him anyway, taking a big sip of wine.

"I have been cooking more these days," he said, proud. He set the dish aside and started separating some of it into plates. "My wife has been very happy. You don't cook much, do you?"

"Not really," she told him. "I find myself not wanting to put time into it when I have other things I'd rather be spending my time on."

"Like what?" he asked dryly.

"Reading books," she said, even though her first instinct had been to say dancing.

"Well, it's not like you're spending your time with someone."

"That was uncalled for," she told him, voice low. She stamped down on her anger; she was too tired to cause a fight. "I went to the date. What more do you want of me?"

"Don't ask me that as if you don't know exactly what went wrong," he admonished without turning around to look at her.

She had had a big Gay Awakening in the middle of the damn date, that was what had happened. But she wasn't going to tell him that. She was barely letting herself think it.

She was here having dinner with him instead of going to salsa, instead of seeing Joanne. She had been cross, at first, when he had invited her right on the day she had dance class, but now she was glad; she didn't know if she could handle it, seeing the other woman right now.

It wasn't like anything had changed—she was just more aware now. But that, of course, changed everything.

"We didn't get along like you wish we had," she said blandly. "You can hardly blame me for that."

"I can blame you for not talking to him properly, not paying attention to anything, and bailing out too early," Beau told her harshly, setting a spoon down with a loud clink against his counter. "You didn't try at all, Bea, which is all I asked you to do. I just worry about you, is that so hard to understand?"

"You don't have to worry about me," she said with an aggravated sigh.

He turned around and gave her a sour look. "You're my little sister. Of course I worry—and not just about your love life! What about your job? Where has your drive gone to, Bea? You had goals, you had energy, you went out and got what you wanted—"

"What I wanted was a small clinic and peace, which is what I have," she interrupted.

"You've settled for a peaceful life," he agreed. "You settled, Bea. Don't you think that's sad?"

She glared at him and said nothing, because she knew he wasn't going to listen, and because part of her couldn't help but think that it was. She knew she was a boring person. She didn't like him rubbing her face in it to punish her for not liking his friend.

"You could have your own hospital!" he exclaimed, throwing his hands up, when she didn't answer. "You could be a surgeon, a head of department, something!"

"So, this is about you being a surgeon and me being a GP," she droned, bored. "Again. I have enough of this from our parents, Beau."

"It's not about you being a GP," he said. "It's about you settling for being a GP and giving up on being anything more!"

"You're not more than me because you're a surgeon," she snapped, standing up. "I didn't come here to listen to this again."

He cursed, reaching for her. "No, don't go! It's just—" He sighed, clearly frustrated. "Look, I didn't know if I should tell you but Carlos is thinking about retiring. He's thinking pretty firmly about it."

"All right?"

"We'll have to look for someone to replace him," he told her. "Carlos was never head of any department, so you wouldn't have too much work, I know you like your peace. But it's a job at a respectable hospital with the possibility of promotions if you suddenly feel like working toward that, and you'd be closer to home."

Bea sat down again.

Beau kept looking at her waiting for a reaction and didn't say anything else, not giving her time to process things.

"That's nepotism," she settled on.

He grinned at her and snorted, quick and amused. She sighed, looking down at the wine glass in her hands.

"I... Why this all of a sudden?" she asked softly.

"I worry about you," he repeated.

She gulped down the rest of her wine and changed the subject. He allowed it, allowed her time to think.

Bea didn't know what to think. She didn't know what she was feeling. She felt vaguely nauseous—but happy, too. Confused. Anxious.

He was still her big brother. She couldn't not be happy that he wanted her close.

****

Bea got home and was thoroughly prepared to take a shower, eat nothing, and spend all night overthinking her visit to her brother and everything her brother had said. She stepped into her apartment already feeling the exhaustion that would crash into her after a long night of no sleep. She let her purse fall to the floor, fishing her phone out of it as she did so, and moved sluggishly toward the kitchen to get herself some water.

She glanced down at her phone and quickly scrolled through her messages.

One made her freeze, one step into the kitchen.

Vivian (salsa teacher): Hey, Beatriz. We noticed your absence today. Jo in particular asked after you and asked me to give you her number, since she doesn't have yours and I can't really give it to her. Hope to see you next week.

The next text was a string of numbers.

Bea immediately forgot about her brother. She forgot about him so quickly it was almost embarrassing.

She stared at her phone, mouth open, and imagined Joanne searching for her in class and not finding her. Was she disappointed? Had she wanted to see Bea? She had asked the teacher to give Bea her number. Bea put a hand over her mouth and felt heat crawl up her face.

She was too old to be feeling like this. She couldn't stop it, though—she had never felt like this.

Christ, all romantic movies had been right. She had always thought they were exaggerations because she had never felt like this before—had never blushed, had never felt her heart beat too fast, had never felt it skip a beat at the thought of someone.

Bea: Hello. This is Beatriz. Vivian said you wanted to talk to me. Thank you for your worry.

She spent nearly fifteen minutes crafting this message after thanking the teacher, sitting on one of the kitchen stools and biting at her bottom lip. She didn't know if she was embarrassed that she took so much time for such a simple message or proud that she hadn't taken longer.

She felt herself flush again when Joanne replied almost instantly.

Jo: Hi! I'm glad! I asked Vivian for your number but she said she couldn't give it to me.

Jo: I guess I thought about asking you if everything was all right and noticed I didn't have your number, so how would we ever be able to talk?

Joanne wanted to talk to her outside of class. Bea felt herself smiling and lifted a hand to her cheek.

Bea: I was having dinner with my brother. If you want, I can warn you when I'm not going to be able to make it to class.

Jo: Mr. Perfect? How did THAT go? And I'd like that. It's not as nice, dancing with the men. You know that if the teachers let us, I'd just dance with you.

Bea pressed a hand to her chest. Her heart couldn't actually be skipping beats, but it felt like it. Christ, she was thirty-eight, not twelve! But it felt…it felt good. To feel like this for the first time. To feel like other people got to feel when they were younger, to have a crush, to have feelings for someone—it felt good.

Bea liked Joanne and she liked liking Joanne, no matter if it worked out or not, no matter what her brother or her parents would think.

Bea: I'm happy for that. It went fine with my brother. I'd rather have dinner with him than be dragged to another stupid coffee date.

Jo: Oh, a date? With whom?

Bea: A friend of his, apparently.

Jo: So it didn't work out, the date? I thought, I don't know, you didn't really go for that kind of stuff. I mean, you said you were never married. But I guess you never mentioned anything. But if it didn't work out…

Bea stared at her phone and bit her bottom lip again. She just brought the date up to see how Joanne would react and she couldn't stop the flare of pleasure she felt at seeing Joanne seem so flustered, even vaguely annoyed.

Bea: It didn't. I don't appreciate my brother meddling in my love life, as inexistent as it is.

Bea: What about you?

Jo: Me? My love life is maybe as inexistent. I've had some boyfriends, but I don't know. It never really worked out.

Bea: I see.

She didn't know what else to say. Her heart was beating like a drum in her chest, her expression, usually bland or blank, now showed all her embarrassment, her pleasure, and her hope.

***

Bea arrived at work the next day earlier than usual, walking slowly and holding a cup of steaming coffee. She had slept well after all, too tickled pink at having Jo talking to her for so long, but they had stayed most of the night speaking and she hadn't gotten too much sleep after all.

"You look tired," Robert said as she approached his desk. He had his eyebrows high on his forehead, his surprise palpable. "Were you out doing something?"

"I always do several things with my day," Bea said.

"Yeah, but you never do anything like going to bars, or parties, or dates," Robert pointed out. "The sort of thing that would keep you up."

"I have been on a date recently."

His eyebrows shot up even higher. "Really? With whom?"

"A friend of my brother's."

He grimaced.

"That about sums it up," she agreed with a sigh. She walked close to his desk and put a hand on top of it, looking around to see if someone was listening in even while she knew that there was no one in the clinic but them right now.

She liked Robert, and she had to tell someone.

"Is everything all right?" he asked carefully.

She sat down on the chair beside him, the one usually tucked in because he was the only receptionist since Maria had quit.

"Robert," she said quietly, "I think I'm a lesbian."

Robert stared at her, then nodded very slowly. He turned more fully to her, hands clasped, and opened his mouth. He closed it again. He picked up a cup of coffee from his desk and drank it all in one gulp, then sat it back there.

"All right," he said. "All right. Why are you telling me this like you just figured it out?"

She stared at him. "What?"

"Bea, I've known you're gay since we met," he told her firmly, looking at her with slightly too-wide eyes.

She gaped. "But I—I didn't know until a few days ago."

"Dude," Robert said with feeling. "That's the—that's the whole reason I never asked you out."

She scratched at her cheek. "Sorry?"

"How could you not know?!"

"I don't know," she groaned. "There's this woman..."

He stood up at once. "There's this woman. All right," he said in a resigned tone of voice. "We're opening the clinic a few minutes late because we're going out to get more coffee now."

She sighed, relief making her droop where she sat. She was glad to have Robert to talk to, glad that she had trusted him and he was apparently worth of this trust. She hadn't realized until she spoke to him how afraid she was that he would have a bad reaction to her words but it wasn't Robert she was really afraid.

Chapter Seven

"Then we'll head straight to Argentina," Carla said, a thoughtful hand on her chin and the other with a finger tracing a path along the world map she had splayed on her bed. It was an old, scraggly thing, and several places in it were colored in—everywhere Carla had already visited. Joanne looked at it and felt something in her heart go tight and hot, something like envy and joy coloring her face red. "We won't have much time, but if we head to the—"

"Wait," Joanne said, sitting up. "You can't do that. You can't leave Brazil without going to the Bird Park."

"I don't care much for birds," Carla said with a shrug.

"Dude!" Joanne yelled, grabbing her friend by the shoulders. "You can't not go to the Bird Park in Iguassu! Are you insane?! It's two hours of looking at macaws and parrots and toucans and—and—it's a huge bird park where you can enter aviaries and take pictures with macaws! You can hold the macaws in your arms like a baby! How can you not want that?"

"How do you know all that?" Carla asked her, eyes narrowed in playful suspicion.

Joanne let her go, embarrassed. "I might have poked around the internet a bit after you guys said you were going there."

Carla laughed. "Jo, you're making me cry! You seem more excited about this trip than I do."

"Well, I finally have someone I can vicariously live through," Joanne said wistfully.

Carla paused and gave her a considering look. But before she could open her mouth to say whatever it was she had in mind, Joanne's phone rang and distracted them both. Joanne looked down at her pocket, blinking, and thought: what if it's Bea?

She fished her phone out of her pocket so quickly that it nearly tumbled out of her hands and straight to the floor. Carla was giggling as she checked the caller's ID, a smile already on her face.

Janet.

Her smile died a sudden, very firm death.

Carla quieted down as well. "What's up? Is something wrong?"

"No, it's just my sister," Joanne said with a sigh. "I thought it was Bea."

She didn't catch the look Carla sent her as she brought the phone to her ear.

"Hey, Janet!" she said with as much cheer as she could find. "What's up? It hasn't been long at all since we've talked. Did something happen? Something better have happened, or else I will hang up, right now."

"I'm in Phoenix."

Joanne's expression froze on her face. "What?" she asked faintly.

"I'm in Phoenix, but I don't know where you live," her sister said tersely. "Give me your address so I can meet you. I got myself a hotel room for the weekend, so don't worry, I'm not looking to mooch off from you."

Joanne stared at the bedsheets in front of her.

"Is something wrong?" Carla asked, putting a hand on her shoulder.

"My sister is in town," Joanne said faintly, and finally realized what exactly she was feeling.

It wasn't shock that had frozen her. No, it was a stone-cold, icy fury.

"Why the fuck are you in town?!" she shouted at her phone. "What on Earth are you doing here? I didn't want you visiting so you said fuck that and decided to fucking come anyway? How do you even know where I am?"

"It's not like you disappeared into the ether," her sister retorted. "One of your new friends posted a picture with you and tagged the name of the bar, it wasn't hard."

Joanne looked at Carla with wounded eyes, feeling betrayed for all that she hadn't told them she was hiding, how would they have known? Carla looked back at her with confusion, with no idea what was happening.

"That doesn't give you the right to just show up here!" Joanne snapped. "I know it's Saturday, but don't you have a life?"

"I need to talk to you!" her sister shouted, sounding fed up, sounding exhausted. "It's not on me you made that as hard as humanly possible! Why can't you stop acting like a child and just come and meet me?"

"I'm going to fucking meet you all right," Joanne snarled standing up. "Go to the bar—the one my friends tagged in the picture. I'm not giving you my fucking address, are you insane? Like I don't know that the whole family would show up at my door the next weekend!"

"The world doesn't revolve on you," Janet said icily.

"You're here, aren't you?"

Janet hung up without another word. Joanne stood in the middle of Carla's room and felt her hands tremble with how much she was feeling, though she wasn't sure what it was: anger, of course, betrayal, maybe, and a bitter sort of sadness. A hint of desperation.

Her escape hadn't lasted more than two months.

"...are you going, then?" Carla asked.

"Yeah," Joanne said. "I'm going. Sorry about that, I didn't mean to spill family drama all over your room."

"It happens," Carla said with a shrug. Then she grinned widely. "Want me to come with?"

Joanne let out a bark of laughter. "No, the last thing I need is you punching Janet in the face in the middle of Jack's!"

***

A part of Joanne hadn't really believed Janet was there, but she was: standing in front of Jack's Spot, with a suitcase at her feet and a tired, beleaguered expression on her face. She didn't look any different than Joanne had remembered, mostly because nearly no time at all had passed since she had last seen her.

Unbidden, under her anger, a muted panic rose.

She hadn't wanted to see anyone. She hadn't wanted anyone to find her, and they did so easily. Was it impossible for her to get away for some time? Would life drag her back by the ankle every time?

"Joanne," her sister said coldly when she approached. "I thought you wouldn't show up, honestly."

"It would serve you right," Joanne said through gritted teeth. "Not only did you fucking come here when I told you I didn't want you to, but you also hung up on me."

Janet rolled her eyes, pushing curls away from her face. "I have an actual serious thing to talk to you about," she said. "Can we go in? Christ, I need a beer."

"What? No," Joanne said with a dry laugh, taking a step back. "I came here to see you so you wouldn't be able to go home and cry to everyone about how I abandoned you; not to go get some fucking beer and let you get away with this."

"Get away? It's not illegal for me to visit my fucking sister, Joanne," Janet snapped.

"I don't want you here," Joanne said as firmly and evenly as she could, willing her sister to understand. "Do you get that? I left because I needed to—"

"The world doesn't revolve around you," Janet repeated, hands in fists. "Just because you did the equivalent of shutting yourself off in your room and locking the door doesn't mean that the world stops turning!"

"I don't care!" Joanne shouted.

Janet's eyes burned. "Our mother—"

"I don't want to know!" Joanne interrupted, squeezing her eyes shut as if that would help her not hear. "I don't want to know; I don't care. Why is it so hard for you to get that I just need some fucking time!"

"How can you say that you don't care?!" Janet shouted. "You don't even know what might have happened!"

"I'm going to leave," Joanne said, because she had hit her limit. She wasn't going to stay here anymore, she couldn't. She shook her head and turned around. "Bye, Janet. Sorry you wasted your fucking time coming all the way here."

"Joanne, our mom—"

But Joanne started running and didn't hear the rest of her words.

***

Joanne was more than glad for salsa that week, since absolutely nothing else managed to get her to stop thinking about her sister and about what it was that Janet could have been so desperate to tell her. Of course she was still angry, still betrayed, but part of her couldn't stop thinking about her sister's words: the world doesn't revolve around you. Our mom—

Spotting Bea at the corner of the room, not on her phone but clearly waiting for her, was such a relief that it felt like pain in her chest. Joanne wasn't shy about dashing toward her and throwing her arms around her waist in a hug, squeezing her eyes and Bea both.

"Um," Bea said, flustered. After a moment, Joanne felt her hands softly on her shoulders, like Bea didn't quite remember where they were supposed to go during a hug.

"I'm so happy to see you," Joanne murmured, resting her head on Bea's shoulder. She hadn't told

60

Bea what had happened even though they had talked on the phone; she had wanted to see her so much, had wanted to tell her in person. Maybe they could get coffee or something after salsa. Bea had liked the coffee date with her much more than the one with that man, after all.

Her eyes snapped open.

"Oh, fuck," she whispered with feeling. A pit grew in her stomach; she felt dizzy. She stepped away from Bea with wide eyes, though she kept her hands at the woman's waist. Bea looked down at her with confusion, a pink flush on her cheeks, and kept her hands on her shoulders too. They weren't hugging anymore, but kind of were, too close for it to be called anything else.

She knew why she had run from her family after all.

"Are you all right?" Bea asked her quietly.

Joanne took her hands away and two steps back, feeling a blush crawl up her cheeks. "I'm fine, I'm good," she said, looking away. "Um. How are you? I was wondering if you'd be okay with, like, hanging out after class? I know it's a bit late, but—well, it's weird to talk through the phone after we saw each other in real life, so I was wondering—"

"All right."

Joanne's eyes snapped up to her. Bea expression was hard to read, since she didn't emote much, but Joanne thought she looked happy.

"All right," Joanne said, feeling suddenly shy.

The teachers turned on the music and the two sprang apart as if burned. They traded a somewhat awkward look. But Joanne was glad for the class starting, glad that she could stop thinking about anything and just dance. She reached out before Bea did, catching her hand and stepping close again.

They danced, fast and happy and laughing, and, for the first time, didn't trade partners once during the whole hour of the class.

***

Joanne sat in Bea's car and fidgeted. The car was old but well-taken care of, and it smelled like Bea. She hadn't realized she knew what Bea smelled like, but this car definitely smelled a lot like her, and her blush just wouldn't go away.

"Is everything all right?" Bea asked softly, like she wasn't sure she should. "You've been quiet today."

And clingy, she knew. But she hadn't managed to keep her hands away after figuring out what she had, and she felt so stupid for not having figured it out before. She ran because she liked women, and she knew her family would hate her for it.

She looked down at her lap and fidgeted with her keys. "I'm fine. I'm good. I mean—my sister visited this weekend, though I guess visited is the wrong word. We had a row in front of a bar, it was very embarrassing. I left home, I left the state, I left for the other side of the country for a reason, you know?"

"Yes," Bea said. "Not the reason, but you did tell me about your leaving."

She parked the car inside the garage of her apartment complex but didn't get out. She took her hands from the wheel and turned to Joanne, eyes dark but bright, all of her hard to see in the half-light of the

62

underground. It made Joanne feel braver, for some reason, the dark.

Bea's eyes were so beautiful. She wondered if Bea thought she was beautiful, too.

"I was in denial, I guess," she said, so quietly Bea leaned closer so be able to hear her. "But I know. I've always known. I just didn't want to see."

"What?" Bea asked, voice just as low.

"They would hate me," Joanne whispered. "If they knew."

Bea just looked at her, hand close enough that Joanne could touch it if she wanted to. She did, so she crossed the space between them and touched the tips of her fingers to Bea's.

"If they knew," she repeated, looking at their hands. "They would hate me. Do you ever figure something out and realize that your whole life was something and you hadn't even realized? Do you ever see, all of a sudden, just how scared you've always been and you didn't even have the guts to see it yourself?"

Bea didn't say anything, but that was fine. Joanne knew that she was an awkward sort of person, when it came to social matters.

"I'm sorry," she ended up saying. "That they don't appreciate you. Or—that they wouldn't. If they knew."

"If they knew about—" Joanne swallowed nothing. She looked up at Bea.

Was that hope she saw in Bea's face?

Bea leaned closer. She was so close. She was so tall and beautiful, her hair falling in front of her eyes as she moved, shot with grey as it was. She was older than Joanne, a competent, successful doctor. The sort of in-law any parent would love to have, if only she were a man instead.

Joanne cupped her face in a hand and breached the space between them, sealing their lips in a kiss.

Chapter Eight

Bea retreated into her kitchen and made coffee.

Joanne was in her living room, wringing her hands and looking around with curiosity. Bea got cups from her cabinets and tried to get a hold on herself. She had never felt like this. Never. She suddenly felt much more forgiving toward her brother's stupidity relating to his girlfriends when they had been younger. She understood now. She felt like she would definitely do stupid things, if only Joanne asked them of her.

She made coffee and pressed a hand to her cheek, trying to control her blush.

"Thanks," Joanne murmured with a smile when Bea handed her a cup. "Sorry for just springing that on you. That was—um. I'd never kissed a woman before either, if that's any consolation."

"I can't believe you just figured things out today and immediately went and—well."

"Kissed you," Joanne murmured.

Bea sat on the couch beside her. Their shoulders bumped together, elbows knocking on each other as they drank.

"I'm sorry about your family," Bea said, heart in her throat; she didn't want to think of her own family and so didn't, at least for now.

"Me too," Joanne said, sounding miserable. "I didn't want to see it, but it just crashed onto me all at once, you know. I couldn't deny it anymore. I guess… I'd never felt safe enough to fall in love, when I lived with my family."

Fall in love. Bea's heart beat a hundred miles a minute. She was surprised it wasn't making any noise as it beat inside her chest. She clutched at her cup and drank the rest of her coffee, desperate for something to say. She wanted to badly to do this right, to say the right thing and do the right thing so she could keep this, but her brain wouldn't help her and her mouth wouldn't open.

When she glanced to the side, Joanne was looking straight up at her. She looked from one of Bea's eyes to the other, then reached for her hand. Bea let her have it, and their fingers twined together.

Maybe, Bea realized, *there's no need to say anything right now*.

Joanne leaned forward and Bea set her cup down beside her, not caring that it might get knocked over. When Joanne cupped her cheek in one hand, Bea closed her eyes and kissed her, softly and unhurriedly. Joanne curved her hand along Bea's jaw, fingers twining on the short hairs on the back of her neck, and Bea felt sweaty and clammy and nervous and a bit like her body was about to burst, almost forty and—

She had been afraid, too, she knew. She had spent her life saying she was content with work and didn't need anyone in her life, and all along she had been afraid to rock the boat; Beatriz had never been in love. Not until now.

Their kiss turned deeper, their lips opening to each other. Joanne explored her mouth with her tongue and Bea felt like a teenager, like she was holding something stolen, something it would be so easy to lose. But Joanne stayed for hours, two hours they spent kissing and holding each other's hands, talking about the thing they wanted to do in the sun.

***

Robert took one look at her and his eyebrows immediately rose up to his hairline.

"You look like you had a nice evening yesterday," he commented, sipping his coffee. His eyes narrowed. "You have salsa lessons on Wednesdays, right? Where you see that woman every week?"

"I did have a nice evening," Bea said evenly, walking slowly toward the reception. As usual, it was early enough that the other doctors hadn't arrived yet, and she had some time to chat with him. She was glad for it, though she didn't care much for his expression right now.

"So….?" She was quiet. He grew impatient. "So, did something happen? Anything at all?"

"Yes," she told him. She willed a blush down—she was in her place of work. Still, she felt something small and giddy yelling joy in her chest. "She kissed me."

"Oh! Holy shit, I didn't think something like that would happen so soon!"

She looked at him reproachfully and he winced. "Sorry," he said. "But you know what I mean."

"I know," she murmured. "I wasn't expecting it either, at all. She just…had a revelation, I guess."

"Wow," Robert said. "I guess you got lucky."

"Yeah," Bea said vaguely, walking toward her office. "I did."

She was lucky. She couldn't deny it. For the first time, she was feeling the full weight of it: that she had met Joanne, that she finally figured out the truth about herself, that Joanne liked her too and had kissed her. She sat down at her desk and looked at her phone; she had a message of good morning from Joanne (which she smiled at and returned) and two messages from her brother.

Her brother, who had offered her an amazing job at a respectable hospital on a silver platter. She was lucky with him too, and suddenly she didn't want to disregard that. Instead of answering his texts, she brought her phone to her ear and called him.

"Beau," she said when the call connected. "How are you?"

"Bea, hi," he said, surprised. "I'm fine, just got back from a run. Did something happen?"

"No," she said, then realized it was a bit of a lie. But she wasn't going to tell him about what had happened; despite her sudden gratitude, she knew he would just double down on his beliefs that her life was spiraling. "I just… I wanted to thank you for telling me about the job. I do appreciate the fact that you were considering me for it. Do you want to get some coffee later today, maybe?"

He was silent for a moment, and when he spoke, pleased surprise was thick in his voice. "Of course, sure! I mean—you're welcome, but you know you deserve it. And I'd love some coffee—Christ, you know I'm here for a few months to talk to that possible sponsor—sorry, can't tell you who—and god help me, I've gotten so tired of having meetings and business dinners every day, all day long."

She smiled. "I can imagine. This is why I chose a small clinic, you know. Let me know when you're free."

"This afternoon is fine," he said, and she could hear him rolling his eyes.

Bea was in such a good mood, she had fun meeting him that afternoon.

***

Bea heard the doorbell and opened her door. Joanne was beaming at her on the other side, her hair a wild cloud around her face and her eyes bright.

"Hi!" she said, stepping in.

Bea closed the door behind her and kissed her. Joanne went on her tiptoes and kissed back, winding her arms around Bea's shoulders and leaning her weight against her. Bea held her weight and tried not to laugh.

"Someone's in a good mood," she commented.

"Someone's girlf—um. Well. You invited me over, so I'm happy," Joanne said, face flushed and suddenly shy.

"Girlfriend," Bea murmured, holding Joanne's hands in hers. "It feels odd, honestly. I'm almost forty and I have a girlfriend?"

Joanne laughed, relaxing at once. "What do you prefer, partner? Like we got a law firm together or something? I'm twenty-seven too and I don't feel weird about saying the word girlfriend."

Girlfriend, Bea thought, and couldn't help but smile. "Come on," she said. "Dinner is almost done. I hope you can swoon at spaghetti and meatballs, because my culinary skills end there."

"Beatriz," Joanne said with patience and amusement, "I've been eating instant noodles nearly every day since I moved here. I will definitely swoon at some spaghetti."

Bea paused. "You should have told me. I wouldn't have made pasta if I knew you'd been eating so much pasta. Also, why?"

"It's easy. Also, my culinary skills end much earlier than yours, at putting together a salad."

"I'll learn how to cook for you," Bea promised her, leading her to the kitchen. The spaghetti was still on the pan with water so it wouldn't get cold too fast, and the tomato sauce was happily bubbling away.

"You are such a romantic," Joanne murmured, herding her against the counter.

It should have been funny, because Bea was a solid half-head taller than her, but Bea felt too flustered not to go where Joanne was leading her. Joanne pressed their bodies against each other and kissed her, catching her hands and twining their fingers.

Bea closed her eyes and kissed back, wanting to sigh, her body fitting Joanne's like a puzzle piece. Their noses bumped against each other but she barely noticed, caught in kissing her girlfriend, tilting her head to deepen it, to taste Joanne as much as possible. Joanne let go of one hand to curl it around her hair, to tug at it, and Bea groaned.

Joanne ended their kiss to press her lips against Bea's jaw, and Bea could do nothing but tilt her head sideways and give her access. She fit her free hand around Joanne's back, then slid it up to the middle of her shoulder-blades, where it was used to resting.

Joanne just breathed against her cheek for a moment, both of them wound up.

Bea kept her close, but stepped forward, and Joanne went easily with her. When she moved a foot forward, Joanne copied her without thinking. Bea stepped back, then leaned away and caught her hand—and Joanne finally laughed.

"There's no music!" she said, face red. But one of their hands was caught in the other's and their feet moved without them having to think about it, music or no music; Bea had them dancing in her kitchen, feeling like the sun had been shoved in her chest. So happy that she felt that it must have been escaping her as sunlight, somehow.

She turned in a circle, Joanne's skirt flaring like a flower blooming, and they laughed.

In the back of Bea's mind, her encounter with her brother lingered. She might have been in too much of a good mood to let the thought percolate too much and ruin her day—her week, her month—but she thought about it anyway: her family would hate her too, if they knew.

She knew, twirling Joanne around in her kitchen and feeling the happiest she had ever felt, that she couldn't let Joanne meet her brother, that the sides of her life could not collide, her overachieving big brother and her bright, young girlfriend.

It was their first relationship, anyway. Neither of them was too serious about it, right?

Chapter Nine

Joanne wanted to shout. She wanted to scream about it, to dance, to sing, to tell someone, but instead she went to her little apartment and stayed alone and kept the knowledge like a well-hidden secret, like a child holding a butterfly where nobody could see it.

She was in love and Bea was her girlfriend and they had kissed and life was beautiful, everything was suddenly beautiful. She went around cleaning her apartment, having to do something, to spend this energy on something. She then called for take-out and stayed up until five in the morning watching movies.

She still woke up feeling rested. She sighed and stared at her ceiling.

"I have a girlfriend," she murmured.

She couldn't imagine Janet's face if she ever learned, much less their mother's or their father's. They all felt so distant, now. She was glad to understand, finally, why exactly she had left, even if it left her feeling quiet and sad. Her ceiling had a big crack crossing it from one side to the other, cutting her room in two.

She could imagine Janet's face, actually. She just didn't want to.

She sat up in bed. Her lovely reverie was broken—she remembered, suddenly, Janet's frantic visit.

Our mother—

Surely… it wouldn't hurt if she just logged on to her social media accounts, would it? She hadn't been checking things ever since she arrived, but she had logged out altogether after Janet told her how she was found... She could just open her phone and check her notifications. Just to see. Surely if anything really horrible had happened to her mom, somebody would have said something.

She breathed in deeply and let it out slowly. She stood up and got her phone from the dresser.

As soon as she logged in, she was assaulted by notifications. She quickly did away with them, trying to find anything relating to her mother. She scrolled through things for a few seconds before she saw something important: she had been added to a new chap group.

The group's name was Friends of Gertrude, who was her mother.

She clicked on it. She read the messages as quickly as she could, skimming them as she scrolled up to the first ones. Something about... exams? It seemed like her sister and her father were asking for money. Joanne felt her heart constrict, but kept on reading before she could draw any conclusions, what if she thought something wrong?

Apparently, the group had been created only a few days after she had left.

Finally, she got to the first message. It was by her sister.

Hey, everyone, she had written. *Sorry to put you all in a group all of a sudden, but it's the easiest way for us to deal with this. I know that some of you already know what's going on, because Mom spoke to a few of her friends about her fears before she told her family everything.*

Unfortunately, Mom's fears were right. She's been diagnosed with breast cancer.

Apparently, it wasn't caught as quickly as the doctors would like it. She's going to run more tests and start some medication and we'll see how things go. This means that we're about to spend a lot of money. I made this group to keep everyone updated and also to ask that whoever can help us, to please do. We'll appreciate anything. Thank you.

Joanne stared.

She stared and slowly her vision blurred, then cleared again when she blinked and her tears fell.

Joanne, our Mom—

Janet had hopped onto a plane and come here when Joanne hadn't wanted to hear her, and still Joanne had sent her away without listening. She had run. She had run, and now her mom was sick and her family was about to be swallowed by medical bills and Joanne was in Phoenix dancing salsa and eating instant noodles instead of doing anything.

Her mom was sick.

Joanne hadn't spoken to her in over three months.

She sobbed. She realized she had been sobbing, suddenly aware of her gasping breaths and the weight of her guilt, and the sheer unfairness of it all. That her mom had cancer and that it had to happen now, that she had ran and tried to have a truer, happier life and this had to happen to fuck it up, and it felt selfish to think it and she thought it anyway.

She had to go.

Janet was right. Joanne felt like she would never forgive herself for not having listened to her sister.

She had to go, to return home and help them with the bills and stop acting like her life was some sort of fairy tale. She stood up and marched to her wardrobe. She caught her suitcase and dragged it out, zipped it open and threw it on the bed. She had no idea what she was packing, only that she had to do it because she had to go.

She didn't have a car and New Jersey was on the other side of the country. She paused when the thought hit her, standing by her bed and clutching shirts in her hands. She needed to buy a plane ticket, which would cost a lot at the last minute like this.

She could deal with it. She breathed deeply, trying to calm herself, and told herself that she was going to deal with it. What was the price of one plane ticket in the face of her mom being sick, even if her savings were dwindling faster than she wanted to think about?

She packed the rest of her suitcase and went to get her laptop, intent on searching for prices.

***

She opened the door for Bea and stepped in, giving her a tight smile. Bea's expression fell and guilt piled on top of guilt inside of Joanne—she hadn't meant to saddle Bea with this, to make her sad as well, but she had wanted Bea so much that she hadn't been able not to ask her to come over. Bea set down take-out bags on top of the couch and hesitantly reached for Joanne, like she wanted to offer comfort and didn't know how.

Joanne's face twisted with new tears and she wound her arms around Bea's waist in a hug. She curled into her embrace as much as she could, sighing in relief when Bea's arms enveloped her. Bea smelled like her shampoo and soap, because she was a doctor and was constantly washing her hands, and Joanne was glad to have her here.

"Tell me what you need," Bea asked in a murmur. "I'll help you. What happened?"

Joanne squeezed her eyes shut.

"My mom is sick," Joanne told her in a small voice. "I have to go back home. But they're all the way in Jersey and I need to get plane tickets and—"

"I'll go with you," Bea said immediately.

Joanne froze.

"Bea, you can't," she said, leaning away and wiping at her face. "We have to be reasonable, you have work, you—"

"It's Friday night, I can go and come back Sunday," Bea told her, hands lingering on Joanne's arms. She had a furrow between her brows, her eyes roaming Joanne's face as if searching for an answer.

"Oh," Joanne said, so full of feelings she wasn't sure what face she was making.

She was going back home, but Bea would go with her. She couldn't believe Bea would do it, would get on a plane and follow her, but she didn't protest again, too afraid Bea would listen.

"All right," she said instead, voice wet with tears.

"All right," Bea said softly, wiping a tear from her face.

Joanne didn't know who leaned forward, but it didn't matter, because they were kissing. Joanne clutched at her shoulders, then at her hair, kissing her and breathing harshly when she could. Bea held her hips in her hands, her fingers sliding up under her loose shirt and creating sparks where they touched her bare skin. Joanne took a step forward and Bea tumbled back into the couch, breaking their kiss to gasp in surprise. She fell, half-sitting, Joanne on her lap.

Her face turned red, but she didn't hesitate to capture Joanne's lips in a kiss again. It was like she knew that Joanne needed this, that Joanne knew she was going to lose this apartment, the dancing and the easy dates she had had with Bea, that real life had come knocking with a vengeance and she was going to suffer and she needed the reassurance of Bea's warm body against hers.

"I've never…" she started.

"We can… We can figure it out," Bea said, sliding her hands under Joanne's shirt until they were high on her back, and Joanne lifted her arms so Bea could shove her shirt off. The shirt ended up on the floor, but Joanne wouldn't give a shit about that on a good day.

Bea's face turned redder and redder, her eyes fixed on Joanne's breasts. Joanne managed a laugh, amused, and kissed her again. Bea lifted her hands hesitantly to Joanne's breasts, growing more confident when Joanne bit her bottom lip and moaned at her touch. Joanne hadn't done anything in so long. She kissed Bea again.

"Here," Bea said, putting her hands on Joanne's hips to push her back slightly. "Get up, sit with your back to me. I think it'll be easier."

"What?" Joanne asked, a bit breathless. But she did as she was told: she stood up and sat again with her back to Bea's front, leaning back against her girlfriend.

Bea kissed the back of her neck. "Here," she whispered, and wound her arms around Joanne from behind, curling her arm around her waist before dropping her hand to Joanne's thigh. She slid it up, bunching up Joanne's skirt, and Joanne's breath hitched.

"It's, um, a more familiar position, I guess," Bea said, shy.

Joanne couldn't really kiss her, so she curled an arm back to touch her face, fingers twining around her greying hair.

"All right," she said, breathless.

Bea did away with her underwear, but kept the skirt, and Joanne laughed. Bea turned red but grinned at her in a way she never had before, pleased and almost fiendish, and when she dipped her fingers between her folds and pressed into her, it hit Joanne all at once: that Bea was here, that she was a woman, that Joanne was leaning back against her breasts and had her fingers in her. She felt present in her body for the first time while sleeping with someone.

Bea slid two fingers into her easily, since she was so wet, and Joanne moaned, throwing her head back onto Bea's shoulder. It was such a simple touch but she felt on fire, a hand digging into Bea's thigh while the other grabbed at her hair, of all her body aware that this was her first time with a woman.

Bea pressed her mouth against her neck, face so hot she felt feverish, her lips full and fervent. She scissored her fingers, cupping Joanne's mound as she moved, her other hand flat on Joanne's stomach, her hands feeling like brands on her skin. Joan breathed harshly, letting her body relax against Bea. Letting Bea do what she wanted.

Bea kissed her neck, then lifted her lips to her earlobe, biting it and sucking it, and Joanne laughed out a moan, happy and so turned on as Bea curled another finger into her. She wound her arm around Joanne's waist and moved her up, just enough so she could get a better angle, and started moving her hand in harsh circles. Joanne moaned, wishing she could just kiss Bea, back arching. Bea curled her fingers in and up, hitting that sweet spot that made Joanne moan her name.

She came at once, feeling almost embarrassed that she had done it so easily, her hands grasping where they could and digging in. Her body felt loose but awake, and she immediately twisted around so she could kiss Bea, grabbing her face with both her hands.

Bea looked at her with wide, wide eyes, her mouth open and her face flushed.

They scrambled away from each other without a word, both thinking the same thing. Four hands tried to open Bea's trousers and they laughed, Bea covering her face with a hand. Joanne grinned, wiping at wetness in her eyes, and opened her trousers, shoving them down. She moved Bea's underwear to the side, not bothering with trying to get them out, and slid three fingers into her at once.

Bea cursed, hips bucking up, a hand grabbing at Joanne's shoulder. Joanne kissed her; they were in sort of a weird position, Joanne perched on the very edge of Bea's knees with her hand buried between her legs, both of them kissing, but Joanne wasn't going to leave Bea's lap ever. Bea didn't relax like she had—

she moved like she couldn't stop it, hips rocking up to meet Joanne's fingers, the tendons of Bea's neck jumping with how hard she was breathing.

She came with a moan caught by Joanne's kiss, her eyes squeezed shut. Joanne's skin rose in goosebumps, looking at her.

Chapter Ten

Joanne lets Bea shower first, for which she's grateful. She spends fifteen minutes under the spray of Joanne's shower mostly staring at the tiles and trying to get a hold on her heartbeat.

She had never felt like that before. It feels incomprehensible that she had spent her whole life alone when it was possible to feel like this with another person.

When it was Joanne's turn, Bea went through the suitcase Joanne had packed and went about folding things and actually packing important things, like Joanne's laptop and her phone charger and a pair of pajamas, and taking out useless things that were just taking space, like the fifth pair of jeans and the plastic bag full of bikinis. It was obvious that Joanne had been very distressed when packing. Bea wished she could straighten her out and make her feel better as easily as she could straighten up her socks.

"Thanks," Joanne said softly when she finished her shower, putting a hand on Bea's shoulder.

Bea smiled at her. "We'll go to my place and pack. Have you looked into plane tickets?"

Joanne nodded. "We can buy them at the airport too."

"All right."

They left for Bea's house.

***

Bea unlocked her front door and stepped in and was presented with the image of her older brother sitting on her couch with a bag of chips in one hand and a book in the other.

"Oh, hi," he said, distracted, when she froze in her own doorway. "I was wondering when you would turn up. It's past six, Bea. We were going to have dinner, remember? Why haven't you answered any of my three thousand texts?"

"How did you get in?" Bea asked, trying to stop her eyes from widening and her heart from beating itself straight out of her chest. Joanne was right behind her, a line between her brows. She looked up at Bea and mouthed a question: who is it?

"The door was open."

"Oh," Bea said. She probably forgot to lock it in her rush to get to Joanne when Joanne had texted her. "It's my brother," she added to Joanne.

Beau finally looked at her. "Do we have a guest?"

Joanne leaned to the side so Bea wouldn't be hiding her from view anymore and waved awkwardly. Beau looked at Bea with a question in his eyes, and Bea, who was too panicked beneath her blank face to make a rational decision, told him.

"This is Joanne, my girlfriend," she said.

There was a pause.

"Like," Beau said, standing up with his face as blank as hers. "Your friend?"

She didn't answer. They stared at each other.

"Bea," Beau said slowly, setting his book down, "what exactly did you mean by that?"

Bea didn't know what to say. She had no idea. She was so deep in panic that she had gone full circle and was feeling pretty calm again. She walked in and closed the door behind Joanne, then headed to the kitchen to get some water.

"Sorry about not answering you," she said instead of answering him. "I'm going to have to cancel dinner; I'm not going to be here this weekend. We can set a date next week. You shouldn't have let yourself in, though. You should have gone back home. Did you have to be so dramatic?"

"Bea, what the fuck did you mean by that?" he asked again, trying to grab her arm. She dodged him and handed Joanne the glass, who took it and took a sip automatically, her eyes veering from Bea to Beau.

"You should probably leave now," Bea said, trying to make her voice firm.

"I'm not going to leave," he said, apparently baffled that she didn't want him here. "We're going to talk about this, because if you mean to tell me that this woman is your—your lover, then—"

"Then what?" she asked. "It's none of your business."

Beau's jaw worked, a muscle jumping on his cheek.

"I said you shouldn't have moved away," he said. "Look at you. Are you serious that on top of everything else, now you've gone this low? You've done this to yourself? I didn't know you were spiraling so much. You should have told me! At least you should have told me that I shouldn't have bothered with Antonio, because you were busy having a fucking lesbian love affair with a teenager!"

"Dude, I'm twenty-seven," Joanne said, disgusted.

"I am not spiraling," Bea said firmly, her hands curling in fists. She didn't want to engage him but she couldn't just let him say those things. She had been so happy—who was he to tell her that her life wasn't good?

"I have never seen a single hint that you were anything but normal," her brother told her, the words like knives. He took a step toward her and Bea froze, not wanting to take a step back.

"This is just a midlife crisis, Bea. Come with me. Really, what do you have here in Phoenix? I will give you that job if you come with me. I'll—"

"Beau, I've asked you to leave," Bea said, her voice cold even though her mind was a churning hurricane of anger and disappointment and longing. She loved her brother. She wanted this job, she wanted to go, she wasn't really happy here, in her clinic and her receptionist as her only friend.

But it hurt, and she wasn't going to give him the satisfaction.

"Bea," he tried.

"I am busy," Bea said firmly. "I've just said that I will be busy for the weekend and that I am cancelling our dinner. You have no more reason to be here, and I am kicking you out. We'll talk later. Goodbye."

Beau sputtered but couldn't linger in the face of her kicking him out so explicitly. They watched him as he squared his shoulders and walked out, his hands in fists.

"Wow," Joanne said.

Bea really had no words. She pressed her lips into a thin line and tried to focus on what Joanne needed, because she didn't want to cry.

***

The next few hours were a flurry of activity. Joanne checked for flights and found a couple that would leave in a few hours, prompting them to quickly pack Bea's things and rush to the airport. Despite the hurry and the awful reason for Joanne's return, her eyes were bright inside the airport, and she was clearly happy to be inside a plane.

"I've always wanted to travel on a plane," she explained once they were settled there and just waiting for take-off. "My coming here was my first time on a plane, this is my second one. Though I wish I were going to, I don't know, South America, instead of back home."

"Maybe someday?" Bea offered.

"Maybe," Joanne said wistfully. "I want to travel. I want to live in different cities, to meet our country and other countries close to us, to not settle. Carla, a friend of mine, is planning this huge trip to the Iguassu Falls in—Christ, in a couple of months, how the time flies. That's the dream, you know. To go out there, to belong to the world."

"Oh," Bea said. "I was never too keen on travelling. I like staying home."

"I guess we're different like that," Joanne said with a smile, though it quickly dimmed, considering the circumstances.

They were very different, Bea realized. Joanne wanted to not settle, to belong to the world.

Even though she was her girlfriend, she preferred to belong to the world, to not be with her, Bea though. Joanne wasn't really serious about them after all—didn't think of them as permanent. Bea couldn't fault her, especially after her brother's stellar reaction. Joanne would be happy out in the world instead of stuck in Phoenix with a boring person like her.

Chapter Eleven

The taxi left them right in front of her home.

It was early morning, now. They had left Phoenix late and arrived in New York, and with the extra drive to Jersey, there was no way they could have arrived at a reasonable time. Bea had found them a small motel to sleep in and they had set out first thing in the morning. Now here they were.

Joanne didn't notice Bea paying or how she got out of the car with the driver to get their bags out of the trunk. She stayed in the back seat and looked at the building in front of them. Home was a small brick building only four stories high. There was a little garden in front of it. Joanne had grown up here, and she was glad in a visceral way to be here, like her body was recognizing that she as home now.

Even so, she also felt a bit sick.

"Let's go?" Bea asked quietly.

Joanne swallowed nothing and nodded.

She walked up to the building and opened the front door with the keys she still had. She rode up the elevator with her girlfriend, and when they got to the right floor—the third one—she walked out and stood in front of her family home. She stared at the door. She needed to knock on it, but her hands wouldn't move.

"All right?" Bea asked, winding an arm around her waist.

"I'm glad to be home, but I really don't want to be here," Joanne admitted. "It's stupid, isn't it?"

"Of course it isn't," Bea said, letting her arm fall.

Joanne knocked on the door. After a few moments, it was opened.

"Milly, we're out of sugar too, I've told you—" Janet started, then froze when she registered who it was that was standing in front of her.

"Hi," Joanne said, shoulders curling in.

"Oh, god," Janet said. "What happened? Are you okay, are you sick? What on Earth are you doing here?"

"So, I saw I had been put in a group chat called Friends of Gertrude," Joanne said, eyes veering away to the floor in guilt.

"Oh," Janet said, then drew herself up to stand straighter. When she spoke, vindication dripped from her voice like honey. "I bet you're feeling really fucking stupid for having ran from me like that, aren't you?"

"There's no need for that," Bea said reproachfully.

"And who's this?" Janet asked, lifting one eyebrow.

"My friend," Joanne said. "She came with me. Will you let me in, Janet? I'm back, I did what you wanted. Can I see Mom?"

"Janet, who's that at the door?" came a faint voice from inside the apartment, and Joanne felt her heart jump to her throat.

She raised her voice before Janet could say anything.

"Mom?"

There was a pause before the sound of someone running reached her, and her mother showed up at the door. Her eyes were wild and her hair thinning, and she looked more fragile, strangely, not like she was physically any different but like Joanne couldn't help but see her like that.

"Jo?" her mother asked, breathless and disbelieving.

"Hi," Joanne said, quiet and ashamed. "I came back as soon as I learned—as soon as I heard. I'm sorry, Mom. I'm here to help."

"You have no job," Janet pointed out with arms crossed.

Their mother didn't hear, throwing herself out so she could hug Joanne to her chest.

"Oh my god," she said faintly. "You disappeared, I thought we'd never see you again. Oh my god, Jo. I'm going to be so mad at you in a few seconds."

"All right," Joanne accepted, hooking her chin over her mom's shoulder and trying not to cry. "I've got some savings, Mom, so I can help you guys, and I'm trying to get a job, as soon as I find something I'll start helping more—"

"So, Janet got through to you after all, huh," her mother said, leaning away. She kept her hands on Joanne's shoulders and examined her face as if Joanne had the secrets of the universe folded between her brows.

"She ran," Janet said, angry.

"She's here now," Bea murmured.

"Come on, come in," her mother said, squeezing her shoulders. "There's coffee, have you had breakfast? Come in. The anger is coming in, Jo, so you better eat something before I start shouting, because it'll be a while before I stop."

"All right," Joanne said with a crooked, sad smile, and they walked in.

***

Her mother yelled at her. Her father grew cold and quiet, which was possibly even worse. Janet stood in the background and looked smug and relieved. Bea sat on the couch with a cup of coffee in her hands and no idea what to do.

Joanne stood in the middle of the living room and couldn't tell them why she had left, nor how long she would stay here. She tried not to talk too much about her life these past months because she knew they would disapprove. She had not tried too hard to find a job and had spent most of her time watching movies, going to bars, and dancing salsa.

When they finally released her from the scolding, she fled to her room and threw herself on her bed, while Bea seemed to be glad for the opportunity to take a shower. Joanne was left alone, staring up at her ceiling of the room she had grown up in. Her posters were still on the walls, her bed the small twin bed she had always had, her childhood plushies on the shelves.

She curled into a fetal position facing away from the door and fished her phone out of her back pocket.

Jo: Hey, sorry for not saying anything but I won't be able to go to the rehearsal Monday, I'm out of town. I came back home to my parents' house and I don't know when I'm going back.

Carla answered nearly instantaneously, and Joanne was glad for the distraction.

Carla: Jo!! Did something happen? Is everything okay? You haven't missed a rehearsal ever since we met.

Jo: I found out my mom has cancer, so…

Carla: Oh shit

Carla: Is she okay? Are you okay?

Jo: Not really. But hey, I have good news. I actually am not straight and have started dating a hot silver fox doctor.

Carla: WHAT?

Carla: JO, YOU HAVE TO TELL ME THAT STUFF.

Joanne smiled. It had been some time since she had spoken to Carla. She hadn't realized how much she had missed her.

Jo: She goes to the salsa lessons with me.

Carla: Oh my god. I KNEW you weren't straight. You couldn't be. Did you know I have nearly zero straight friends? Statistically speaking, you had to be a lesbian.

Jo: LOL.

Jo: Tell me about the trip?

Carla: If you talk to me about your awesome silver fox girlfriend. We're still settling some things! It's awful trying to coordinate hotel rooms and whatever we might visit when you're in a group with several people. But we think we have a hotel picked out, so things are going smoothly.

Carla: Speaking of settling things, I wanted to know if you're still trying to find work as an editor. I remember you talking about it some time ago.

Joanne blinked in surprise.

Jo: Yeah, definitely. Especially now, what with how much money Mom's about to spend.

Carla: Then I have a guy whose information I'll send you. A friend of a friend or something. He's got a small publishing press, I think, and wanted to hire some editors to help him.

Jo: Thanks, Carla!

Joanne sighed and turned around, staring up at nowhere. Honestly, the idea of settling down with a job right now didn't appeal to her at all, but what else could she do? She quickly managed to turn the subject back toward the trip and let herself get distracted with dreams of the falls.

***

Bea sat down on the bed beside her, putting a hand on her shoulder. Joanne turned on the bed until she was on her back gazing up at her girlfriend. Bea looked more settled now she had taken a shower and had some coffee, for which Joanne was grateful; one of them had to be well.

"What do you need?" Bea asked softly.

Joanne lifted her hands to Bea's face and brought her down into a kiss. The door to her room was closed, so one kiss couldn't hurt, even though people weren't shy about barging into rooms here. Joanne swallowed her fear just for now, fingers twined on Bea's hair.

They let their lips slide off each other slowly, ending their kiss. Bea leaned to the side and laid down beside her, her head on the pillow but most of her body out of the small bed, both her feet on the floor.

"I have to go at best tomorrow afternoon," Bea said.

"I don't know when I'm going back," Joanne admitted in a small voice.

Bea paused. "What about your apartment? How long does your lease run? And you left a lot of things behind."

"I know. But, how can I leave again, Bea?" That was the crux of the matter: Joanne had left once and look what had happened. She was afraid, in a small, childish part of her, that if she went back to Phoenix something else horrible was going to happen.

Bea didn't say anything. She didn't look like she was pondering an answer or desperately trying to find something to say—she looked like she knew, and understood, and that she hated it, and that she didn't want to say whatever words she had trapped in her mouth.

Chapter Twelve

The rest of the day was quiet, and so was Sunday. Joanne's mother had grown too tired of fighting, though her father was a quiet man and hadn't even started yet. Her sister Janet kept swinging between annoying Joanne as some sort of revenge for having left and growing quiet and sad. Bea was thoroughly out of place in there, and she could admit that she was relieved to go back home.

She couldn't put her life on hold for Joanne. She had the clinic, her brother, a decision to make about moving away from Phoenix to go work at her brother's hospital, and Joanne was too occupied with her mother and her family and her returning home to be able to pay attention to any of that. That was fine. People had lives. But it still made Bea feel lonely.

"Call me when you get to the airport, get on the plane, and when you land," Jo said, standing with her at the front door and trying to block her curious family with her body. She was failing; she was short, and Joanne's mother was looking at Bea with undisguised curiosity over her head.

"All right," Bea said softly. "Call me if—anything."

"Everything's going to work out," Joanne said with a tired smile. "I'm going to figure things out. Sorry I can't go with you. Mom asked me to help her with sorting some documents to take to the hospital—"

"That's okay," Bea interrupted her. "Stay with your family. We'll… We can talk later."

"All right."

Bea wanted to kiss her but couldn't. It chafed at her, left her feeling raw and small, but it wasn't like she could say anything—it wasn't like her family was any different.

She squeezed Joanne's hand for a second and walked away to the taxi.

They hadn't spoken about what this whole mess meant for their relationship. They hadn't spoken about what Beau said and offered, about the fact that Bea might just move away, too. Joanne had so much going on—but there was the fact that what they had was so new, too. It all felt so fragile. Bea was afraid. Was it really so easy for life to get in the way of things?

***

Bea arrived home late on Sunday and was glad when she walked in that her brother wasn't waiting there like a very unwelcome surprise again. She had a small dinner and fell into bed, not wanting to linger too much on things that had already been percolating in her mind during the entire weekend. She was glad that the next day was a Monday and she had work to go to.

Robert took one look at her face and set his coffee down.

"Hey," he said. "Everything all right?"

Bea paused. She looked at him and sighed, then walked up to his desk and sat down on the second chair.

"Some stuff happened," she said.

"Like what?"

She sighed. "My girlfriend might be moving away from Phoenix and back to her parents' house in

95

New Jersey. She wants to help her mom, who found out she has cancer... I just... I guess I understand, but I'm still sad that it was so easy to leave me."

"Well, she's helping her mom," Robert said.

"Jo's always speaking about moving away, though," Bea said softly, looking down at her hands. "She talks about wanting to see the world, wanting to live in several different cities, about not wanting to settle. I guess I was just surprised at how quickly she moved away from me, no matter the reason."

"I guess that is a pretty different life than the one you have," Robert said. "You're very quiet and settled...but look, I know this is like your first relationship or something—it's normal, all right? No matter how much you love a person, sometimes things just don't fit. Sometimes you want different things, or you're in different stages of your life. You'll meet new people, all right?"

Bea frowned. She hadn't expected him to say that—that she should just accept that Jo was leaving and that she was going to meet new people someday. She felt sad. Was that how normal people thought? Was she wrong to get so attached so quickly?

...was Jo, despite her words (in love), someone who thought the same as Robert, who thought that they should move on with their lives and leave each other behind? Would it be so easy for Joanne to leave her, after all?

"I'm sorry, either way," Robert added when the silence lingered. "I don't mean to say that you two are going to break up. She's there for her mom, right? Maybe she'll come back. Maybe she'll take you with her if she travels around."

Maybe, Bea thought. *But probably not*. it wasn't like she had ever spoken to Bea about Bea coming with.

A part of her thought about how new their relationship was and how normal it was that they hadn't spoken about anything serious—but Bea wasn't so young anymore. She wasn't in a stage of her life where she would want to dawdle and date for years before letting things turn serious.

A part of her—small, heartbroken—thought about her brother, about his offer, about what her own parents would think, about Joanne's parents and the shitshow that it would be, their lives colliding.

Bea checked her phone. She sent the messages to Joanne, telling her she was home, but Joanne hadn't answered.

She didn't want to, but a part of her thought it anyway: *maybe it's for the best that it happened soon, since it'd spare me more heartbreak.*

It wasn't like she thought Joanne was going to ignore her forever and abandon her, but she knew just how easily people could draw apart.

***

Bea waited for him in front of his huge apartment, standing in front of the gates while he took the elevator down to meet her. The night was cool—for Phoenix, anyway—and she didn't mind staying down here. She didn't want to go up to his apartment. She hadn't forgiven him, and she wouldn't for a long time. But Bea had thought about some things: about her future, about how happy she really was in Phoenix, about how easy it had been for Joanne to upend her life and why it felt so, so hard for her to do the same, and she had arrived at a conclusion.

"Bea," her brother said, stepping out of the gate and into the streets with her. "Why are you making me come down to fetch you for? Did you forget the way to the elevator? Let's go up and have something to eat."

"No," she said simply. "I don't want to go to your place, and honestly I don't want to talk to you. But I thought about the things you said and I've reached a conclusion, and I didn't want to tell it to you through the phone."

His eyebrows rose. He was quiet, waiting for her to continue with his arms crossed.

"If you are still offering the job at the hospital, I am interested."

His expression shifted to one of shock. "What?"

"I am interested," she repeated. "I am not happy at the clinic. You're right. It's too small and too quiet, even for someone like me. My only friend is the receptionist. I would be glad to be in a hospital with many doctors, nurses, and others to talk to. And I'd like a change—both personally and professionally. I've been at the clinic for many years."

He gaped at her. "I... I mean, all right, but what brought this change of mind?"

She paused in thought. She thought about Joanne, fleeing to Arizona from New Jersey with some savings and nothing else aside from confidence and joy, and how easy it had been for her to go back home. Travelling around the world wasn't as hard as she had always thought.

She shrugged.

They were silent for a moment.

"About the last time we saw each other," Beau said carefully, "and your, uh, that woman. Does this mean you two—"

"What we are or not is still none of your business," she said blandly.

His expression closed. "So, you come asking for a job but won't let me ask a single question, me, who has only ever worried about you and how you're doing."

"You're the one who offered the job," she pointed out, keeping her voice even. "Also, I know what you're going to say and I still don't care for it. If you want to rescind your offer because I won't break up with my girlfriend, then that's on you. There's nothing I can do."

Beau looked away. "At least you'll be closer to home. Closer to your family. Then maybe things will go back to normal."

She just looked at him evenly. She didn't want to argue, mostly because she knew she would not convince him.

She felt good about her decision. She felt settled, like something anxious inside of her had finally calmed down. She had stood still and done nothing for far too long—it felt good to decide something. She would talk to Joanne about it later, but there probably wouldn't be any problem. After all, Joanne was the one who moved away from Phoenix first.

She wondered, looking at her brother and thinking about how easily Joanne fled from her own family, if Joanne would ever suddenly cut contact with her.

Chapter Thirteen

Joanne didn't really leave her room when she wasn't out having dinner with the family or helping her mom with something. She didn't want to linger in the living spaces and have to weather her father's and Janet's silence, or her mother's small but constant barbs. So, she went when required and stayed in her room otherwise, scrolling through her social media apps on her phone or rereading the teenage romance novels she used to read—Christ, upwards of ten years ago.

Bea didn't really text her after those first few texts. Joanne knew she was busy with her work and didn't want to bother her. She texted Carla instead.

Jo: I can't believe I used to read this. I think I could write something better if I wanted to.

Carla: LOL then do it.

Carla: Speaking of! You got an interview! The guy liked the resume you sent him, he said he was going to email you soon. You owe me so much, Jo. Next time you're in town we're going out for drinks and it'll be your treat.

Jo: You get me a job so you can make use of my money, I see.

Carla: Hell yes.

Jo: But really, thank you. I guess I wasn't looking for a job at all while I was there. It's really biting me in the ass now. When my parents ask me what I was DOING, what can I tell them? Going on shows and getting drunk?

Carla: And making out with a hot doctor?

Jo: I'm not gonna tell them THAT.

Carla: That sucks. But hey, tell me how the interview goes. At least SOMETHING'S going right, right?

Jo: Yeah.

It was a few minutes later that the email arrived, and she was surprised at how quickly the man wanted an interview—they were going to make a video-call and chat for a few minutes and then she would be hired or not. Apparently, the last editor left without a word and the work had accumulated very quickly. As a freelancer, Jo was going to earn by project, not by the hour, so the amount of work made her happy.

It wouldn't tie her down anywhere, a job like this. A part of her was happy about that, but most of her didn't know what to think. Maybe it would be easier to go back to Phoenix if she had had a job there—but then, the thought of being tied to anywhere made her feel slightly sick.

She wanted to feel free again. She didn't even want to open the door of her own room, here.

***

Joanne dashed down the stairs and rushed to the living room, where her mom was knitting and Janet was watching TV. They both looked up at her as soon as she appeared, surprised that she was out there with them instead of inside her room. She smiled at them.

"I got a job," she said with a grin.

"Finally," Janet said, then looked back at the TV. She was trying to feign boredom and disinterest, but Joanne could see right through her—she knew Janet was happy.

"Finally," their mother said, relieved. "I'm going to admit, living in here with one less paycheck hasn't been the best thing in the world, what with how much money we've been spending..."

"It's going to be all right now," Joanne said firmly. "I'm not suddenly rich, but the contract he's drawing up is for a year of employment, so we don't have to worry about that for a year. And it's not like I can't find other clients."

"Sit down here," her mother said softly, so much so that Joanne couldn't say no. She walked forward and sat beside her mother on the couch. Her mother sighed, patting her hand before catching it between both of hers. "I'm glad you're here to help us again. But... can you really not tell me why you left? I keep wondering why, because if I don't know the reason, I can't know when you're going to do it again."

"I'm not going to do it again," Joanne said, looking away. She still felt guilt, but also sorrow, that she really would never again have the life that she had had away from here.

"How can I know that?" her mother asked, voice small.

But Joanne couldn't tell her. She looked in her mother's eyes and she knew that this would eat at her mother forever unless she told her, but she also knew that her mother would hate her if she knew. Maybe not in a shouting, kicking her out kind of way. But in all the ways that mattered, her mother wouldn't love her anymore.

It was the worst thing in the world to know that.

***

"Hey," Joanne said, voice so low it was almost a whisper, curled up in her bed under her blankets. After the heat of Arizona, New Jersey felt positively frozen to her. It was a nice excuse to keep herself hidden and protected like this.

"How are you?" Bea said softly. "It's been some time since we talked."

"I'm good, I got a job as an editor," Joanne told her. "Carla helped me—you know my friend, the one with the band? It's a one-year contract, so that's some time I won't have to worry too much about finding work. How are you?"

"Good," Bea said, then there was a pause. "I've accepted my brother's offer. I'm moving to California to work at his hospital."

Joanne's mouth fell open. "What?"

"I need a change of scenario," Bea said quietly. "I'm too isolated here. I was afraid too, Joanne. It took me a long time to realize that, that I had done what you did, just…more slowly. But I don't want to be afraid anymore, and I don't want it to affect my life like this. I'm going to get a job at a big, respectable hospital, and meet new people, and see my parents for the first time in almost six years."

"But," Joanne said. "But Phoenix? We're going to be so far away with you in California."

"We're already far away," Bea pointed out. "You're in Jersey, after all…unless you're coming back?"

"I don't know," Joanne said honestly.

She had no idea if she was staying here or going back. Living here would mean not paying rent—but she had the contract that tied her to her Phoenix apartment for the next couple of months anyway. But that would mean staying away from Mom and staying away from this mess. But would it just be running away again?

She had no idea. She didn't want to think about it.

But she missed Bea like a wound, missed dancing and Carla and the shows and the bars and the fairs, missed everything that wasn't here.

And now Bea was the one moving away. Not that Joanne was surprised—Bea was so good and competent, a good doctor, and she deserved to work at a place with a name, somewhere where people would appreciate her properly, no matter how much of an asshole her brother was. Bea deserved it, so Joanne couldn't say anything.

She wasn't surprised that Bea would want a better life, either way. That she would want something better than staying with someone with unstable work like her, who never went to college and still lived with her parents, who felt anything but like a good and competent anything.

Chapter Fourteen

Bea went to salsa class that week, mostly because she was still paying for them, no matter how much she didn't want to right now. It was the one thing she did that got her out of the house, and she was desperate to do something. So, she went. She instantly regretted it.

The room was wide and white and open and everyone saw her when she walked in, turning to her in surprise.

"Beatriz, I'm glad to see you. Neither you nor Joanne answered my texts after you missed class last week," Vivian said, crossing the room to greet her. "Where's Joanne? Is everything all right with her?"

"There was a medical emergency in the family," Bea told her. "I'm sorry for not answering. I hadn't even seen that you sent something. But we're fine."

"All right," Vivian said, sensing that she didn't really want to talk about it.

Another student called her and she went easily, nodding at Bea one last time. Bea was left alone in the back of the class, and out of habit she got her phone. She didn't really know the other students, not the men she had danced with in the beginning nor the women she had danced with before Joanne had taken her and refused to dance with anyone else.

She stood there and wondered why she had come. It had been stupid to start this class anyway. What had she thought? That salsa was going to suddenly make her an extrovert with lots of friends and fix everything in her life?

At least Joanne was coming back later to get the rest of her things from her apartment, and maybe Bea would feel a bit better.

***

Joanne opened the door for her with a relieved smile and only barely waited until they were inside before she pressed Bea against the door and kissed her. Bea felt tension leave her shoulders as she wound her arms around Joanne's waist and kissed back. She had missed her, and she hated not knowing when they would meet again. She was glad that Joanne had asked her to help her pack, because at least she would see her.

"Thank you for coming," Joanne said fervently. "I know I'm staying there, but god it is unbearable. I don't think I've done anything aside from lying in bed and reading books since I arrived."

"Some people would really like to do that," Bea pointed out.

"Not me," Joanne grumbled, stepping away and heading to the kitchen. "I was about to ask Carla if I could go along on her trip to the Iguassu Falls and now this. I'll end up never leaving that house, Bea. It's going to drag me back."

"Wait, what trip?" Bea asked, blinking in surprise…and hurt. "You didn't tell me you were planning on any trips."

"Carla and some friends are planning a trip to South America," Joanne explained, not even looking at her as she shoved canned food out of the cupboards and threw them on a box labeled to donate. "Carla tells me all about it and I really want to go. We haven't known each other for a long time, so I was a bit shy about asking, but I wanted to! I wanted to go."

"You didn't tell me," Bea repeated, and remembered speaking to Robert, wondering if Joanne would bring her along.

Apparently, not only would Joanne not bring her along on her adventures, she didn't think to even tell her about it.

"It's not like I'm going," Joanne said, turning around with a confused frown. "Are you…upset about this?"

"I don't know. Were you just going to come to me one day and be like sorry, I'm off to South America for I don't know how long, see you later? What if you ended up talking to your friend about it and deciding to go—when exactly would you tell me about it?"

"Well, it's not like you can come," Joanne argued. "You have a job."

"I can take vacation days," Bea said slowly.

"Would you?" Joanne asked dryly. "Would you even want to come? You're—well, you're not exactly an adventurous person, Bea."

"Yeah, I guess I'm too settled for you," Bea said, the words slipping out before she could take them back.

Joanne stared at her. "What's that supposed to mean? I know my situation isn't exactly stable—"

"I'm not talking about that," Bea said.

"Aren't you?" Joanne said, and now she sounded angry. "I know you're a big shot doctor and now you're moving to work at a huge, fancy hospital, but that doesn't mean you're better than me!"

"I didn't say that, don't put words in my mouth," Bea snapped. "I know I'm a boring person, all right? I knew you wanted to travel the world and live everywhere and, I quote, not settle, and that I'm the most average, unexciting person in the world—"

"When have I ever said anything like that?"

"—but I thought that at least you would tell me when you planned your wild trips—I thought you maybe would want to take me with you."

Joanne stared at her, mouth open. Bea could see it written on her face: she had never considered that Bea could want to go with her. She, when daydreaming about her wild adventures and her perfect life, had never imagined Bea by her side.

"I guess it doesn't matter anymore," Bea said. "I mean, you've already left."

Joanne winced as if Bea had shouted. "I haven't left. You're the one who showed up out of nowhere and told me you accepted your stupid brother's invitation, that you're moving to California. It's not like you talked to me about it either!"

"Would it matter? You left first."

Joanne looked at her with a wounded expression on her face, her eyes wide. Her mouth worked for a second; she was trying to find her words. Bea waited, looking around the small apartment. It was taken apart—Joanne really was leaving, and so easily. So quickly. Such little time they had had together.

It really was easy for things to draw them apart.

"So, you just...left too?" Joanne asked quietly. "You saw that I—because of my mother—that I was going away, and you decided that, all right, you might as well leave too, no use trying anymore? Had you meant to leave all along?"

"You're the one who never meant to stay," Bea said. "I knew you would leave eventually; you always talk about being a free spirit, about not wanting a job tying you anywhere, about having a free life. I don't have a free life, Joanne. I have a very settled life. What was I supposed to think?"

"So, I'm going back to Jersey and you're moving to California and...that's that?" Joanne asked quietly.

"Are you going to tell your family about us?" Bea asked, sad and betrayed. "Would you ever, had you ever planned to? Phoenix was a fairy tale for you, Joanne. Real life has come knocking, and I'm part of the fairy tale. Unless you plan on telling your family—"

"I can't."

"Then what are we supposed to do?" Bea asked quietly. "See each other twice a year, and even then, lock ourselves in, hoping that nobody sees us, stealing moments like we're fifteen? I'm almost forty."

Joanne didn't have an answer to that. God help her, Bea didn't have one either. If this was where the world was leading them, what could they do.

"I'll help you pack," Bea said. "Then..."

"I think I'd rather you just left now," Joanne said quietly, voice wet.

And Bea couldn't stay after that.

Chapter Fifteen

"What the fuck," Carla hissed.

Joanne curled up on Carla's bed and buried her face in a pillow, too tired and heartbroken to even accept the ice cream her friend had bought her. She was glad that she had Carla, here; she didn't know what she was going to do when she went back to Jersey.

Bea was right. This had been a fairy tale.

"I can't believe she broke up with you!"

"She didn't exactly break up with me," Joanne said.

"She did," Carla said, fervent. "You went back to Jersey for your mom, and she was upset that you didn't invite her on a trip you weren't even enjoying?"

Joanne smiled. It did sound a bit stupid when put like that, but she knew that there had been a lot of things under what actually happened, thoughts they had both had since the beginning that had come bursting out. She couldn't blame Bea for not thinking Joanne was serious about her. Joanne didn't know what she wanted. She had no idea what her life was going to be.

"It was more than that and you know it."

"Fights are never about what people are shouting about, are they?" Carla said with a sigh, resigned. "I remember one time me and Jacob were fighting about how I never buy him gifts, and we ended up both crying about our fathers."

Joanne didn't want to think about her father.

"I can't fault her," she said quietly. "I have no idea where my life is going and she wants something more stable. Something better than this."

"Nothing is better than you," Carla told her firmly, holding her hand and squeezing it. "You and she might have your differences, but that doesn't mean she's better."

"All right..."

"And don't go disappearing on me when you're back in Jersey, all right?" Carla said, straightening up. "If you do, I will pull a Janet and show up to shout at you in front of a bar. I'm gonna be honest, at the time I was pissed, but right now... I really would do the same."

Joanne laughed, but at the same time her heart felt constricted—was Carla afraid that she was going to disappear, too? Joanne had never meant to make the people she loved feel like this.

***

Joanne went back to her parents' house and managed to sequester herself away in her room by saying she had to work. The excuse had the nice aside of being true; Joanne sat cross-legged on her bed with her laptop on her lap and went about earning some money.

She wondered what Bea would have said if she had found a job before any of this could happen, if she had found something stable and respectable. The thought made her wince, but looking at the pages and pages of fiction she had to revise and work on, she winced as well. It was boring work.

She didn't know what type of work she wanted, but the thought of staying in the house all day, every day, just typing on her laptop made her feel slightly sick.

But what else could she do? She wasn't qualified for any other type of work, really, and she needed money fast to help her mother. She could think about wild trips and a free life or anything like that. Medical bills could break people. She needed to help.

She stared at her laptop's screen for a long time before she started to type.

***

Joanne heated up some instant noodles. There were leftovers for dinner and even frozen meals on the freezer, but Joanne wanted something to feel the same as it had in Phoenix and this was the only thing she had found. While she heated up water, Janet made herself a fancy salad and toasted some bread, all the while giving Joanne dirty looks.

"Do you think you're seventeen instead of twenty-seven?" she asked as Joanne poured boiling water into her noodles cup.

"What, because your dinner is the healthiest thing in the world? You're just trying to lose weight."

Janet flushed with anger. "I'm acting like an adult, unlike you. Not only did you run away like a teenager, you came back with your tail between your legs and now you're eating instant noodles and locking yourself in your room all day!"

"I came back because I learned my mother is sick," Joanne said, baring her teeth at her in a smile.

"I tried to tell you," Janet said, the force of her hurt and her furry shining through the words. "I spent money we desperately need right now to go to you and tell you and you ran. You ran."

"I'm sorry," Joanne said, looking back down at her cup. Her guilt grew and nearly swallowed her, and it made her curl her shoulders in.

But Janet didn't care.

"You can't just do that," she said. "You fucking can't, Joanne. We have no idea what you were doing there, what people you were with, if anything happened—and you won't even tell us why you left in the first place! You say you're back to help mom, but what guarantee do I have that you're not just going to fly out to fucking Los Angeles next week?"

"I'm not!"

"What guarantee do I have?"

"I came back," Joanne snapped. "That's your guarantee—I came back the second I learned something was wrong, the moment I heard what had happened! Do you think I'm going to ever be able to run away like that again? After what happened this time, after learning that my mom had cancer and I didn't know for months and it was my fault? What sort of person do you think I am?"

"I don't know," Janet muttered. "I don't understand you anymore. And who was that damn woman you brought with you? She looked much older than you and she told Dad she's a doctor? Where did you even meet her?"

"Salsa class," Joanne told her, a frown on her face. She didn't like Janet's tone, like she was being dismissive of Bea. They had broken up, but—it was still Bea. Joanne didn't like Janet talking about her like that.

"So, you were off having salsa class," Janet said. "That's what you were doing. You were dancing salsa and making friends with—whoever the fuck that weird woman was—"

"She's not weird," Joanne snapped.

"She looked like a man," Janet said, voice dripping with judgement.

Joanne felt her hands closing in fists and her mouth opening, even though she really, really didn't want to say what she was thinking.

"Admit that you realized she's gay," she said, "and that's what got you hating her."

"I don't hate her," Janet said defensively. "I didn't want to assume; you know that's rude. But it was obvious! We've all just been wondering why you brought her here, into our house, and why you're friends with someone like that!"

"Someone like that."

Janet paused. "A homosexual. You know what I mean!"

"I brought her here because she was my fucking girlfriend," Joanne snarled before she could help it, helpless fury and panic boiling inside of her. She slammed her hand down and didn't notice her dinner spilling all over the counter.

Janet stared at her, mouth open, frozen in shock. She looked away from Joanne and then back at her like it would make a difference, like she could blink and Joanne would be back to normal.

"You mean she... Christ, what did she do to you?" Janet asked at last.

"She didn't do anything," Joanne said. "You wanted to know why I ran? Here's the reason."

"You ran to go off be with some woman?" Janet asked, back to furious; anger was easy, anger was easier than having to deal with this. "You left us all to have some sort of weird relationship to this woman who's much older than you, who none of us know—are you telling me that she made you go?"

"She didn't make me go!" Joanne yelled. "I didn't go be with her! She didn't do anything to me, Janet, I've been gay all along!"

Janet clearly didn't know what to do. She made a face of disgust.

"You are—"

"Yes, me! I'm gay! A homosexual! A lesbian who likes women and wants to sleep with women—"

"Don't tell me that!" Janet shouted. "Jesus Christ, Joanne, are you out of your damn mind? Be glad our parents aren't home right now to hear all this! You need to stop this nonsense and come back to planet Earth! You're not a fucking lesbian, you idiot, you just want attention—"

"Do I want attention? Look me in my fucking eyes and tell me I just want attention," Joanne said dangerously.

Janet grew quiet. And then, slowly, she grew horrified.

"Joanne, you can't mean that."

"I do."

"You can't—it can't be true. We've never seen any hint—you're not like that. You can't be. You're—you're normal."

It broke her heart. Joanne stood there in the kitchen and felt hurt like she never wanted to feel, the exact hurt she had been running from when she left. Janet was looking at her like she didn't know her, like Joanne was suddenly a stranger instead of her little sister.

"I am normal," Joanne said quietly.

"At least the woman went back," Janet said, relieved, for all that she took a step back—away from Joanne. "You're home now, and everything's going to back to normal. I tell you that Julien has some friends I could introduce you to. You just need the right man. I'm telling you. You're not—you can't be."

Joanne looked away from her and finally realized she had ruined her own dinner.

She had been wrong to leave like she had. She knew that now. It had been wrong to go away and cut off contact, to try and isolate herself entirely from her family, to try and avoid this—there was no avoiding, and she only created problems and stress for everybody. For the people she loved.

But it hadn't been wrong to leave.

She wasn't going to live with this, she knew. Janet's disbelief would harden into disgust sooner rather than later, and once she realized Joanne wasn't backing down, she was going to tell their parents, and god knew what would happen then.

It hadn't been wrong to go to Phoenix, but it had been wrong of her to abandon everyone. She's the one who made Phoenix into a fairy tale, and it was never going to last. It hadn't been fair to Bea. She got it now. Bea hadn't been wrong to feel unsteady with her, to simply believe that Joanne was always going to leave her.

But Joanne could do better now. She wasn't running again but leaving didn't have to be running.

She could do better.

Chapter Sixteen

Bea didn't go to salsa the next week. The thought of going was too depressive—the thought of having to dance with other people was strange and saddening and it wasn't like it mattered, since she would be moving away and would stop the classes anyway.

The next day when she arrived at work, Robert took one look at her and sighed. He pushed back the chair beside his and slid a cup of coffee toward it. Bea sat down gratefully, giving him a tired smile.

"Did something happen?" he asked.

Bea was so grateful for him that she slid the coffee back toward him. She didn't know how else to show him just how glad she was not to be alone, that she had him—and she had had him all this time, hadn't she? Robert was a better friend of hers than she had thought.

She remembered thinking of him as just her receptionist and contained a wince.

"Not really," she said. "I've already told you that she broke up with me. Yesterday I didn't go to salsa class and I guess it just made me sad."

He patted her shoulder in sympathy. "I'm sorry. Have you spoken to her at all since it happened?"

"No," Bea said with a sigh. "It's understandable. Why would we talk? She's in another state, on the other side of the country. It wasn't like it was ever going to last, anyway. You yourself said that there are other women around..."

"I guess," he said. "But...I'm sorry anyway. Why do you say it wasn't going to last, though? You seemed so happy."

"Jo wants to be a free spirit, wandering around the country and living life to its fullest, traveling to other corners of the world. She wasn't ever going to settle with me. It makes me sad, but...I always knew."

Robert furrowed his brows, a thoughtful look on his face.

"I mean—did she tell you she was only interested in a casual relationship?"

Bea's brows were the ones to be furrowed then.

"Not really," she admitted. "We didn't really talk about our relationship, I guess. She...she said she was in love with me, once. On the very first day. But she always said she wanted to travel."

"Wait, so you didn't tell her you wanted a serious relationship?"

"We didn't really talk about it," Bea repeated with a shrug. "And I knew from the beginning—"

"How did you know?" he interrupted, giving her a look. "If she didn't say, if neither of you commented on it, if you didn't talk?"

"We're not children," Bea said, a bit annoyed. "We don't need to talk about every little thing. It was obvious."

Robert looked at her with—was that pity? Bea bristled at the sight of it, but most of her was worried about what exactly made him have that expression.

"Bea," he said, "did you ever wonder how things might have gone if instead of assuming your girlfriend wasn't serious about you, you had asked her about it? Asked her to stay with you, told her that you wanted her close, that you wanted something lasting, instead of letting her go?"

Bea stared at him.

"I..." she tried. "It wasn't—I didn't... I knew she wasn't going to stay, so... She never considered taking me with her, so—"

"Yeah, but did you tell her you wanted to go?"

Bea stared at him in silence.

"God, you useless lesbian," Robert said with a groan. "Just call her!"

"She's in another state!"

"And they don't have phones there?" he asked her dryly. "Look, I love you. You're a good friend, you're like the one person in this place who actually asks about my book and takes the time to chat in the morning. So, take it from me: call her, and you can fix it. This isn't some type of over-dramatic rom-com or something. You can just talk to her."

But Bea couldn't. Robert didn't know—he only knew what she had told him and he didn't know everything. He didn't know about her brother, about California, about Joanne's parents. If he knew...

But he was right, wasn't he?

"I don't think she would want me back," she said quietly. "She let me go."

"You let her go too," Robert said kindly. "It goes both ways, a relationship."

Bea paused.

"How's your book, by the way?"

He rolled his eyes, but he was smiling. "All right, I'll let you get away with changing the subject. But think about it, yeah?"

***

121

Bea watched as her brother pulled something that smelled amazing out of her oven. She was sipping some wine and he was chattering about something, about his wife and children and his dog and work and she wasn't even pretending to listen. Things were stable between them, mostly because her brother had returned to normalcy with a single-mindedness she didn't know he possessed and both of them were pretending absolutely nothing had happened.

He set a plate in front of her.

"I think you'll like it," he said, pleased.

"We've broken up," she said, and only realized that she said it once the words were hanging in the air between them.

Her brother had a face like he had just stepped onto droppings in the street. He straightened up. She looked evenly up at him.

"Good," he said.

She threw the wine at his face.

He sputtered, shocked, taking several steps back. "What the fuck, Beatriz?!"

"She was my girlfriend and I love her and that's what you say," she said evenly, though her hand was closed in a fist. "You have the fucking gall to come to me and say *good*. Who do you think you are?"

"Why did you tell me, then?" he demanded. "I thought, what with you accepting the job offer and coming to California, that you'd broken up with her because—"

"We broke up for reasons that are none of your damn business," she said, then sighed. "I don't know what I expected. Maybe I just wanted some sympathy. Maybe I wanted a hint, any hint, that you weren't asking me to go with you to the hospital because you want to fix my life, but because you love me and you want me near. I'm such an idiot."

"I do love you and want you near," he said, wiping wine off his face with a scowl. "But Jesus, Bea, was I supposed to be sad you broke up with that woman?"

"I'm sad," she told him quietly. "I love her. For the first time I was with someone I actually wanted to be with. I know who I am and what I want and you, you're looking at me like I'm a stranger."

He was quiet for a moment.

"Bea, once you're home, everything is going to be all right. You can put this behind you and nobody has to know. Look, you're a smart woman. You know it's...it's not natural. Our bodies were made to—"

"Don't preach to me about biology, Jesus Christ," she said, wishing she hadn't thrown her wine at him. She wanted to gulp it down.

You studied medicine too," he said.

"Yes, which means both of us know that nature and biology don't care at fucking all about our prejudices."

He sighed. "Look—does this mean you're not coming to the hospital?"

She looked away.

She still wanted to go. She had made a decision and she was going, because she thought she could be happier there than she could be here. She still loved im. She still wanted his approval, his respect. He was her older brother. It hurt her that he was saying those things to her face and hurt her even more than she wasn't even surprised.

"I'm going," she said softly. "I'm going because I think I can be happy there. I'm not going for you, Beau, and I'm not going to do anything you ask me to or want me to do. I'm not going to owe you. You offered and I accepted. That's it."

He sighed but didn't argue. They finished the day mostly in silence.

***

An hour after her brother left, she heard a knock on her door. She, who had taken a shower and was lounging on her couch trying to read a book and not to think of anything, stood up slowly. Maybe he had forgotten something?

She really wasn't looking forward to seeing him again. She unlocked the door and opened it slowly, trying to peer through the gap to see if it really was him.

Joanne smiled awkwardly at her and waved.

"Hi."

Bea shoved the door closed.

She stood in front of it and gaped, heart racing. Joanne was here? Joanne was here? What was Joanne doing here? It was nearly eight already. Why was she here now?

"Bea?" came Joanne's hesitant voice from outside.

Bea put her face in her hands and tried very hard not to feel happy, utterly happy that Joanne had come to her.

Chapter Seventeen

When Bea managed to open the door again, she felt more composed. She had kept Joanne waiting for a bit, but Joanne didn't seem to mind; when she caught sight of Bea, she smiled with relief.

"Sorry for just showing up," she said quietly. "I can go if you want me to, I know it's late."

"No, it's all right," Bea was quick to say. "Please, come in. Do you want coffee?"

"Please," Joanne said, looking relieved that she had asked; she looked tired.

Bea retreated into the kitchen to make coffee and give herself some more time. When she came back, Joanne was sitting on her couch and staring at the pictures around the TV stand in front of her, eyes glazed.

"Here," Bea said, handing her a cup. She sat on an armchair adjacent to the couch instead of beside Joanne. "Is everything all right? Did you need anything?"

Joanne looked from the cup to her, eyeing the distance between them like it was offending her, though her expression cleared when she looked up at Bea.

"Yeah," she said. "I guess I… I talked to my sister and it got me thinking about some stuff."

Bea froze. She couldn't mean that she thought her homophobic family was right, could she?

"You were right," Joanne said, and Bea blinked at her in surprise. Joanne smiled at her expression. "I did make Phoenix into a fairy tale, and that wasn't fair to anyone. Not to my family, not to you. Especially to you. I'm sorry. I didn't...I didn't even think about it, at the time. But you were right. I'd never meant things seriously. I knew I was living on borrowed time."

Joanne waited for an answer. Bea winced and tried to say something.

"I'm sorry."

"Me too," Joanne said softly. "I should have been clearer—"

"I should have talked to you," Bea interrupted before she could lose her nerve. Her knuckles were white around her cup of coffee. "I should have told you I wanted things to be more—that I wanted things to be serious. That I loved you, that I didn't want things to be so...fragile. I just accepted that they were and did nothing and...and it led us here."

Joanne was quiet for a moment. "I really had never thought about asking you to come with me," she said.

"I had never thought about asking you to take me along," Bea said. "Even when I wanted to go."

"Bea, can we make this work?" Joanne whispered, setting her cup down on the coffee table between them. "Can we try? I feel so stupid. It all feels so stupid. I told Janet about us, you know, the way I told you I never would be able to, and it was just...it was sad but it was easy. It was easier than living a lie. Can we try? I...I'm thinking about coming back. I shouldn't have left the way I did, but I don't think leaving was a mistake. I really can't live like that."

"I'm sorry," Bea said, not sure what she was feeling: some fervent, bright and hot combination of feelings that was making her feel like someone had hidden the sun in her chest and it was giving her an awful fever. "I shouldn't have just—I can't complain about you not including me in your plans and then go ahead and decide to move to California without saying anything."

"That's fine," Joanne said a bit wetly, giving her a hopeful smile.

"All right," Bea whispered.

They looked at each other for a moment, separated by space and a coffee table. Bea wanted to touch her so badly that her hands were tingling.

"This feels a bit…" Joanne paused. "Anticlimactic."

Bea laughed. She opened her mouth in a grin and laughed the way she almost never did, reaching for Joanne's hand across the oceans between them and twining their fingers. Her smile was slightly desperate, because she still felt like it would be easy for things to fall down around her ears, but—she felt good.

She felt good.

"Yeah," she agreed. "But that's—that's life. Life isn't grand gestures and wild confessions and—it's none of that, is it? Life is sitting down and talking and figuring out what we did wrong."

It was understanding that you weren't a saint, that you made mistakes. It was going through the horrible, heartbreaking process of accepting that people wouldn't change for you even if they loved you, of accepting that you have to apologize, that nothing will change if you don't. That it's easy for you to stand still and let things go, and so hard to decide something, to go through with something, to take a stand and refuse to move.

Bea felt her eyes shining with tears, because she had wanted this all along, and she loved that Joanne had given it to her. That Joanne loved her. Because Bea didn't care about wild gestures—she had just wanted this. A quiet, honest conversation. An understanding.

That's life. That's love, too.

Joanne smiled at her, then tugged her forward. Bea went easily, willingly, because no one would have been able to stop her going to Joanne right now. Joanne kissed her wrist and sat her on her lap, and Bea smiled. She was so much taller than her like this. Joanne sighed and buried her face in Bea's neck.

"I did make a grand gesture," she complained. "Didn't I hop on a plane and travel here from the other side of the country?"

"You did," Bea said, amused, and then realized: she really had. Joanne was probably having to save as much money as she could to help the house and her mother, but she had come anyway. She repeated, this time more heartfelt: "You did, Jo."

Joanne's arms tightened around her waist. She leaned away from her so she could tip her chin up, and, feeling like her heart would burst with it, Bea obliged her with a kiss.

It took two seconds for the kiss to catch on fire.

Bea felt all of the past few weeks of stress and sorrow and doubt and just plain sadness melt away and coalesce into something that could only be called need. Need to have Joanne close, to have this. She closed her hands in fists around Joanne's curls and went easily when Joanne turned her around and dropped her weight down until Bea was lying on her back on the couch, her legs around Joanne's waist. They just kept on kissing, lips sliding against each other wetly and noisily.

Bea didn't know how, but soon their clothes were off and somehow, they didn't stop kissing through it, didn't stop touching each other for a second. Their clothes were thrown to the floor, forgotten. Joanne lifted her hands to her breasts and palmed them with confidence, making a moan slip out of Bea. She held Joanne by the shoulders, her knees around her waist. A foot of hers slipped out to the floor and she didn't even notice, both of them in a precarious position in the small couch.

When Joanne started kissing her way down her chest, Bea gasped. Her skin rose in goosebumps, everywhere Joanne touched her on fire. She couldn't believe Joanne was doing it—she knew men usually didn't like it, or so she had heard so often, but Joanne looked at Bea with confidence and a smile.

She parted her with a finger and fit her mouth around her clit.

Bea moaned, back arching. And, shit, Joanne knew what she was doing—not because she had done it before, but because she was a woman and knew what she liked. And she wasn't shy, though her face was flaming red: she used her lips, her tongue, sucking her clit and dipping her tongue inside of Bea until Bea was breathing harshly and clutching at her hair, staring at her with wide eyes.

"Bet no man ever made you feel like this," Joanne said with a smirk.

Bea laughed. Joanne laughed with her and came easily when Bea tugged her up into a kiss, their bodies fitting together like puzzle pieces. Joanne fit a thigh between hers and Bea sighed in satisfaction. She grabbed Joanne by the hips and rocked up against her thigh, relieved at the friction against her clit, marveling at the feeling of Joanne rocking against her own thigh in turn. They thrust up and down against each other, breaths mingling as they kissed.

They came at the same time, fingers digging into each other's skin and lips sealed together in a kiss.

***

Bea woke up to a mug nudging her shoulder. She blinked her eyes open and saw Joanne with a hesitant smile, holding coffee and sitting by her hip. Bea smiled at her, happy, and beckoned her down for a kiss. Joanne laughed quietly and obliged her, her curls forming a curtain around them both.

"Morning," Bea said.

"Do I catch a hint of smugness in that voice?" Joanne asked playfully.

"I do have a beautiful woman bringing me breakfast in bed," Bea said sitting up. "Plenty to feel smug about."

"This is just coffee," Joanne said, a bit shy.

"Thank you."

Joanne looked down. "Will you drive me to the airport later?"

"Do you have to leave now?" Bea asked. "Could you stay a couple of days more? I mean, if you don't have a job…"

"I do!" Joanne told her, brightening up. "Carla helped me—I've been hired as an editor, it's a freelance position but the contract is a year-long one, so that's that. Though…since it's freelance, it's not like it matters where I am. I could postpone my return. I don't want to go back," she admitted.

Bea winced. "Do you plan to…just come back here?"

"No," Joanne said. "I can't do that again. I mean—I can come back and live here, but I won't disappear like that again. And it doesn't make sense for me to stay here when you're in California and Mom's in Jersey, does it?"

"It does if you want to be here."

Joanne gave her a smile. "It mattered that I left, not where I went. So, Phoenix isn't really… I really have no reason to be here. Aside from free tickets to Carla's shows," she added with a laugh.

Bea sighed, catching Joanne's hand in hers. "I don't want to see my family in California either. It's been a long time since I've done more than call my parents, and I have no illusions as to how they'll take the news that I'm not straight. But I don't want to isolate myself here anymore. My brother…"

Joanne winced. "Did he say anything else?"

"Yeah, but, he helped me see some things, too, I guess. I don't know."

They were both quiet for a moment.

"I guess we both have to talk to people," Joanne said. "To try and settle things as much as we can."

"Yeah."

***

131

Which was why a few hours later Bea called her brother and asked if he wanted to come over for brunch. He accepted easily, which was a surprise, and arrived late, which kind of was, too. When he finally knocked on the door, Bea had started nibbling at the pancakes and Joanne had given up on trying to impress, having gone to sit on top of the table. She was wearing a shirt of Bea's and rocking along with whatever music she was listening to on her earbuds.

"It's open, come in," Bea said.

Beau walked in and froze, eyes wide. Joanne lifted her head and smiled a grin that Bea had seen before, and it took her only a second to place: that grin she had smiled in class when she had been defending Bea's right to dance whatever steps she wanted, like she knew she was right and was daring anyone to try and argue with her.

"Hi," she said.

"Beau," Bea greeted evenly.

"You didn't say she was going to be here," Beau said.

"Oops. I made pancakes. They are already cold. Why are you late?"

Beau shrugged, still eyeing Joanne suspiciously. "Bea, can I talk to you for a second? In private?"

"No," Bea said. "Let's have brunch, and if you can't behave in front of my girlfriend then I will kick you out, and that will be that."

"Didn't you tell me you two had broken up?" Beau asked, exasperated.

Bea shrugged. Joanne smiled at her and kicked at her lightly.

Beau's eyebrows furrowed at the scene. "Bea, I don't know if I'm...uh...comfortable. With all this."

"I called you here because I wanted to talk," Bea said. "Even if I think that there's not much I can say, I guess I wanted to try again. I'm not going to be able to change your opinion, and I know I definitely won't be able to change our parents' opinion—"

"Oh, god, you don't mean to tell them, do you?" Beau asked, horrified. "Bea, you can't do that. You'll break their hearts, you'll ruin the family, you can't just—"

"I'm not going to hide," Bea said quietly but firmly. "That's what I brought you here to tell you. I'm not going to hide. I'm going to live my life. And I'm not going to isolate myself or push anyone away, Beau. If I'm distant, then that will be your doing. I'm not...unnatural. I'm not weird, or broken, or being tricked, or having a crisis, or trying to get back at you in any way. I'm happy, finally. Do you understand?"

He pursed his lips and said nothing, looking from one of them to the other. Bea hoped he saw how happy she was, how much she loved Joanne, she hoped he saw that she was all right. She couldn't know for certain, but she hoped.

"I guess we'll see how things will go," he muttered at last.

"Yes," Joanne said. "We will."

Chapter Eighteen

Janet called when Joanne was making dinner that night. She was still at Bea's, mostly because her apartment didn't have anything in it anymore. She didn't stop stirring the tomato sauce and Bea looked up curiously but continued carefully snapping the spaghetti in half.

Joanne just looked at her phone for a moment before she brought it to her ear, keeping it balanced between her head and her shoulder.

"Hey, Janet," she said.

"You said you were coming back yesterday," Janet said, worried and annoyed that she was worried. "I guess you at least answered the phone this time."

"I've extended my visit," Joanne explained. "I sent a text."

There was a pause.

"I haven't gotten anything."

"That's not my fault," Joanne said. "I did send it."

"I guess you at least answered the phone," Janet muttered. "When are you coming back?"

"In a couple of days," Joanne said. "Work isn't an issue since I do home-office, so… And I can't keep paying for plane tickets, so I probably won't come back for some time. Better stay here as much as I can."

"You're with that woman, aren't you?"

"Yes," Joanne said. "I'm with my girlfriend, yes. Janet says hi, Bea."

"Hello," Bea said.

"Bea says hi," she told Janet.

"I did not say hi to her," Janet said annoyed. "Look, Joanne. You know Dad's not going to let you back in the house if he learns of this. Let's just be honest, okay? He won't. So, either you stop this stupid business, come home, and go back to living your damn life, or—or I don't know. You'll have to find your way. Mind, Mom will probably be sad, but...she won't dispute Dad's decision."

"I know," Joanne said, and managed to even keep her voice steady.

She knew. That was why she had left.

"What about you?" she added.

"Me what?"

"Would you dispute Dad's decision?"

Janet was quiet. "Just figure out your damn life," she muttered.

She hung up. Joanne didn't know what to make of that, but she had come to accept that she wouldn't ever understand some people and would never change their minds. She would figure out her damn life and live it best she could.

Bea wound an arm around her waist, pulling her to her side in a hug. She pressed a kiss against her forehead, and the two of them thought about their families, and about having only each other, and tried to be okay with that.

***

"Jo," Bea said, though she didn't look away from where she was folding Joanne's T-shirts to put them back in her small bag, "you told me your sister said

135

your parents are likely not to let you in if and when you tell them the truth."

"Yeah," Joanne said, sat down on the bed and playing games on her phone, because her girlfriend was doing her packing for her.

"Would you...stay in Jersey, then?"

Joanne finally looked up at her. "I don't know," she admitted. "I mean...maybe? I wouldn't stop sending money to Mom. I...I can't, even if they do kick me out, if they... I have to help her. So, I don't know if I'll be able to leave, especially if I do find some other job."

It took Bea a long time to speak again.

"I'm looking for a place in San Francisco," she said. "Just know that you'll always be welcome there. If you want to go."

"Oh," Joanne said.

Bea's words unfurled the future to her like a flower blooming: suddenly, Joanne could see it, see them, together in another city after all this was done, her parents far away and Bea's parents—who knew how they would react and how things would go. But Joanne could see them happy in there, together and working and travelling together and going to dinners and dancing.

Bea looked back at her with a smile, and Joanne smiled back.

***

"Just stay in Phoenix," Carla begged, holding her hand. They were at the airport and Bea had left to get them all some snacks. "Just stay! Your apartment is paid for at least another month and you can totally renew that, and I'll—fuck, I'll help you with rent if you need!"

"Carla, don't make this harder than it has to be!" Joanne exclaimed.

"You're our greatest fan, the shows seem so empty without you there," Carla said, teary-eyed. "Who is going to cheer us up during rehearsals? Who's going to shamelessly buy our shirts and strong-arm strangers in bars into buying them too? Fuck, at least go to New York instead of Jersey."

"I feel offended. I was born in Jersey, you know."

Carla sighed the sigh of the suffering. "At least we'll see each other in January."

Joanne lifted one brow. "Are you visiting me in Jersey, then?"

"No," Carla said, then grinned at her. "I'm getting you a Christmas present early, since you won't be here to receive it on the actual date."

Joanne blinked at her. "What? Carla, it's not even close to Christmas."

Carla just shook her head and pressed an envelope into her hands. Joanne gave her a look but went to open it obediently. A long, thin, rectangular piece of paper fell out. Joanne squinted at it for a moment before the words she was reading actually registered in her mind.

It was a plane ticket. JFK-IGU, it said, as well as other information Joanne slowly took in, such as departure: 9h00min, seat F23, January 23rd.

"What?" she said, looking up at Carla with tears already in her eyes.

"I know you really can't afford a trip right now, especially with the way you've been traipsing around Arizona and Jersey these days," Carla said. "We pooled some money, there's many of us, it wasn't too expensive. You're gonna have to bank the damn Bird Park on your own, girl, but the rest we've got covered."

Joanne's vision blurred with tears. "What?" she asked, disbelieving, clutching the ticket in her hands.

She couldn't believe it. Carla couldn't have done that.

"We wanted you with us," Carla said. "Everybody misses you, you know. Next trip, you can pool some money to help somebody else. Somebody always needs help. I mean, usually not to this extent, but you know."

Joanne looked down at the ticket in her hands.

It was real.

She was going to visit the falls and the bird park and Brazil and Argentina. She was going to travel. She was going to leave the States.

She started to cry, her face screwing up. She lifted a hand to try and stop it, but she couldn't—but Carla didn't mind. Carla hugged her tightly, and let Joanne close her eyes and be filled with joy.

Epilogue

Two months later she was in Phoenix again, which surprised nobody. Carla shouted at her for making her feel that they would never see each other again, but Joanne told her that she could hardly control when her girlfriend was going to gift her with surprise tickets to another state.

The reason Bea insisted on her coming was their teachers had arranged a dancing lunch of sorts: they had reserved a huge table for their students at a barbeque place that also had live music, the owners of which were their friends. After lunch, a space would be cleared where the students could actually go and dance outside of a classroom.

Joanne tried to dress up, though she wasn't the kind of woman to care much about that. Bea put on an honest-to-God suit, making Joanne feel a bit faint and rather like she wanted to stay home, preferably in bed. They went together, surprising no one apparently, and chatted with some people during lunch. They had never made many friends among their fellow students, but it was strangely nice to meet everybody again.

Then it was time to dance. Bea reached for her hand and Joanne accepted it, and when they stepped onto the dance floor no one would be able to tell that it had been months since they had last been together. Their bodies flowed like one, their hands clasped and their legs moving in synchronicity, and the smiles they had on their faces were identical: huge and filled with happiness.

They danced the whole afternoon together, never taking their eyes off one another.